They come to Amberleaf Fair, toymakers, storytellers, conjurers and adventurers. They bring song and dance, gifts of love and tales of far places. But in the midst of the celebration, the high wizard Talmar is stricken with what appears to be the Choking Glory, his brother Torin the toymaker has been rejected by his lady love, Sharys the conjurer, a fabulous necklace from across the sea has been stolen—and Torin's the chief suspect.

This year Amberleaf Fair promises to be more than a place of marvels, a crossroads for magic, mysteries, and fabulous wealth. This year the fair promises to be much more interesting...

AT AMBERLEAF FAIR

Phyllis Ann Karr

ACE FANTASY BOOKS
NEW YORK

This book is an Ace Fantasy
original edition, and has never
been previously published.

AT AMBERLEAF FAIR

An Ace Fantasy Book/published by arrangement with
the author

PRINTING HISTORY
Ace Fantasy edition/November 1986

ISBN: 0-441-52009-X

Ace Fantasy Books are published by The Berkley Publishing Group,
200 Madison Avenue, New York, New York 10016.
PRINTED IN THE UNITED STATES OF AMERICA

One

TORIN'S BROTHER TALMAR was probably dying. Beautiful Sharys planned to accept a marriage toy from Valdart instead of Torin. The toy involved, a rare pendant from beyond the western ocean, had either disappeared from Valdart's tent overnight or been transformed into a citron. Likewise, Talmar's magic globe had disappeared from his tent to appear in Torin's. Since Talmar's own charms protected both his tent and Valdart's from thievery, it looked very much as if Torin, born to magic-mongering though trained by his own choice in toymaking, were the likeliest intruder. All in all, East'dek's Amberleaf Fair had not begun auspiciously.

In order of time, Sharys had dropped the first of these rockslides across the path up the toymaker's mountain of life. She had come to his tent yesterday morning as he was setting up his booth.

For half a year, Torin had always kept one toy close at hand but never displayed for sale: a woman and a man no larger than his thumb, completely separate yet clasped irremovably together in each other's arms, carved without the use of joint or glue from a single piece of cherrywood. When he glanced up and saw Sharys standing before his showledge, his hand went to this carving in its padded bag even as he asked, "Aren't you helping prepare the students' banquet today?"

"Oh," she said, "I have only the cold transformations. The fresh fruits and cauliflower and the rest. Mother's doing the wines and Grandmother's doing the hot things, except the soups. Mother and I are making those out of the vegetable water when it's boiled, but we won't do that until the very last. . . ."

Often throughout the summer and early autumn he had almost brought the toy out of his pocket, but left it there after all because he could not think of appropriate words. Now, on impulse, he gathered his courage and pulled out the bag.

"Torinel," she said, "don't."

He hesitated, then put it on the showledge between them.

She picked it up, opened the bag, drew out the entwined statuettes. After gazing at them for a moment, she returned them to the bag, pulled its drawstrings tight, and handed it back to him. "I've been afraid you would. That's why I wanted to tell you at once. Brother Torin, last night Valdart offered me a marriage token, and this morning I decided to accept it."

He had not thought of this chance. Not even though he had been close friends with Valdart since they were children together and with Sharys since she was a child, and should have been able to guess something of their souls. "You've hardly met him," he said at last.

"I met him three years ago, when he came to visit you in spring and stayed until it was almost too late to travel again."

"But you were still a child then."

Sharys smiled. "Most people will probably say I'm still a child now. But you don't believe it." She glanced at the marriage toy in its bag. "Torinel, I've thought about this all night."

If he could call her still a child, he would have been able to touch her hand. "Sharilys . . . think about it longer. This year he'll stay until spring. But he has no craft except adventuring, Sharilys. One winter out of four or six—at most—a few days some stray spring or summer, otherwise you'd raise your saplings alone."

"With my mother's and grandmother's help."

"Since the spring Valdartak and I were twelve years old," said Torin, "I did not see him for twenty years, until he came into my shop three springs ago."

Sharys touched Torin's hand. "I'll think about it until the last night of the fair. But would you truly want to marry into a magic-mongering family, Toymaker?"

She pressed his hand and left. As he watched her walk away, slender in her light green conjurer's robe (so nearly the traditional color for all children before their first name-lengthening), he became aware of movement beneath his fingers. He lifted his hand and saw it had come to rest on the bag with the marriage toy. His face grew a little hot.

"Well, best quiet it." Dilys the storycrafter had approached his booth from the other side. Her holiday tunic was so covered with embroidery as to appear almost a solid whorl of color.

"I didn't hear your walk," he said.

"Which may be why you usually lose a toy or two from your showledge every fair."

He coaxed an awkward smile to his face. "Or I may accidentally transform them into life more often than I realize so that they stroll away and lose themselves."

"I doubt that."

For the length of a few breaths they both looked down at the small, wiggling bag. "We've talked this through before," Dilys went on at last with a sigh. "When you've accidentally lent it an extra measure of animation, it is not killing to transform it back into what it was."

"But it needs more concentration." Covering the bag

with his hand again, he closed his eyes. His thoughts were harder to align than usual, but eventually he felt the double statuette quiet once more into carved wood. He wondered how much Dilys had heard. Although she had become like a sib to him in the ten years of their friendship, there were conversations one would not want even a parent to over-hear. He lifted his hand again to let her see the naturally unanimated bag.

She touched it, looking a hint regretful. "You're not the first person who's had to step out of the light and allow the one you'd choose to make a different choice, Torinel," she remarked. "I've crafted stories about it. Maybe you'll close your booth early and come hear me tonight?"

"Yes . . . maybe, if you avoid telling stories about mar-riage," he half promised.

"I'll devote the whole evening to the cycle of Ilfting the Dwarf."

But as it happened, he had to close his booth early for another reason.

The East'dek area fair was rather small, coming near the end of the autumn festival season. This Amberleaf Fair, only seven scholars had sat down to the traditional first-day banquet for members of their class: Vathilda, Hilshar, and Sharys, the hosts, and Talmar—four magic-mongers; La-deran and his apprentice Iris—two skyreaders; and one judge, Alrathe.

Until his fifteenth spring, when after much delving into himself he left magic for crafting, Torin had shared the scholars' banquets. Sometimes, when business was slow at such hours, his thoughts still returned to nostalgia and the present meal behind tent curtains held stiff with a spell. But this afternoon his mind had hardly glanced at the ban-quet, engaged as he was with Kara and Ulrad.

Both were far-traveling merchants, and both had re-turned this autumn from the south, though by different routes. Kara made a three-year circuit, Ulrad a two-year. Kara was tall and thin. She dressed like most crafters hereabouts, in colored trousers, light tunic, and holiday cape. Though she lacked a star on her cheek, people sometimes mistook her for a magic-monger. Since magic-mongers varied as much as anyone else in body, Torin thought the effect came from her gaze, at once distant and inward-seeming. One of her donkeys carried nothing but her own clothes, so that wherever she went she could adopt the local fashion.

Ulrad carried fewer clothes but boasted that he wore only what pleased him best, wherever he was. Somewhere his clothes might blend into the crowd, but Torin suspected that they looked more or less outlandish everywhere in Ulrad's round, so that he always made himself a walking sign of his trade, like Dilys with her heavily embroidered holiday tunic. Ulrad's choice of style, however, was puzzling. Most of his garments were meant to fit his body rather close, but that body fluctuated by as much as two or three dozen pounds between seasons on the trail and seasons in well-populated places, so that the garments rarely fit as they should. When Torin had seen him in Horodek at the start of this year's autumn fair season, he had been thin from the long journey and his clothes hung loose; now at the East'dek fair the toggles looked about to tug free from his vest and the seams of his breeches appeared in some danger.

Having missed Horodek's Amberleaf Fair, Kara sought out Torin's booth on the first day of East'dek's. She was not pleased when Ulrad bustled up and began to make his new selection before she was finished making hers. "I think you've already had the choicest picking in Horodek town," she observed.

"Ah!" Ulrad chuckled. "But this lad's crafty. He doesn't spread all his best work out at the big fairs. He always saves some for the small ones."

"Not the best tradecraft," Kara replied. "Nevertheless, even if this were the season's only fair, I have earned the earlier choice."

"It's a long season," the toymaker put in, "with time to

craft new pieces between each fair. Why not both choose at the same time? But in case you both want the same toy, Kara takes it."

Ulrad grunted. "No matter if my trade pieces are more to your own liking, Toymaker?"

"No matter." Torin was almost as proud of his business scruples as of his quality craftwork. Besides, after trading in this area ever since the Horodek fair, Ulrad should have more local moneygems than exotic trade pieces, so this time the toymaker planned to make him pay in money-gems.

As they picked amongst the toys in the general display, Kara and Ulrad probably suspected that Torin did indeed always try to keep fine pieces in reserve, some for farm-crafters with late harvests and folk with homes on the farthest rim of the neighborhood, who could come only to the smaller, later fairs; some that he would offer first to certain friends and old customers; some that he would put out only on the last day, so that local buyers would always have as good a chance as eager tradecrafters.

Far-traveling merchants, who were as much adventurers as tradecrafters, developed different ideas about good business. Torin theorized that it grew in part from the difficulty of determining fair prices between area and area, and in part from the inconvenience of carrying the same wares indefinitely. Had he shown these two his entire stock, Kara might have left some fine toys for local customers, but Ulrad would have tried to buy up all the best at once, lecturing the toymaker that it was to his advantage to sell as quickly as possible. Kara, at least, kept her suspicions to herself and did not try to argue settled crafters into dealing by the rules of her own poetry of life.

Still, it soothed a toymaker in his thirty-fifth autumn to be sought out by traveling merchants and to consider how traveling merchants had been seeking him out since the first season of his independent craftworking only ten years ago, and in how many far places toys marked with his birdlike "T" were already prized and praised. So musing,

he almost brought out the marriage toy for their consideration.

No. Not yet. Had Sharys told him after the day's work
was finished, or had Dilys not interrupted his despair at its
very start, he might have flung that toy into the fire. After
half a day of selling new toys and accepting old ones to
mend at free moments during the fair, he had begun to tell
himself that when Sharys actually coupled with Valdart
would be soon enough to burn his own token. Or sell it to a
traveling merchant and let it be carried far away where its
next buyer would see only the fine craftwork without
guessing the personal pain. For it was an exquisite piece of
carving. . . .

Ulrad's hand and Kara's landed on the same toy at almost the same moment. They stared at each other, and
Kara said, "How much, Toymaker?"

"Which is it?" Torin reached down to move aside their
covering fingers.

Ulrad tightened his grip. "Not until you've noted that
my hand touched it first."

Kara lifted her hand from his and smiled. "Take care
you don't damage it for me. How much, honest Torin?"

Reluctantly, Ulrad let it go. Torin saw it was the statuette of Ilfting the Dwarf and his pet porcupines, inspired by
a story Dilys had invented. "Three pebbles."

Kara nodded. "Three pebbles is the accepted price hereabouts this season for a quart of southern brandy, two for a
yard of thick silk, one for a citron."

"My citrons brought two pebbles apiece at the Horodek
fair," said Ulrad, "and the last of them would have brought
two and two-thirds here, if you hadn't come with a donkey's load of the fruit to thin its value." He looked at Torin.
"But they say, Toymaker, that you can be more than half
magic-monger when you choose, and make your own
tongue pleasers out of rocks and twigs once you have the
pattern. You'd rather have honest moneygems now, I
think?"

Torin would indeed have preferred Ulrad's moneygems

to Kara's trade wares, but he disliked Ulrad's practice of
raising his price for delicacies as his stock diminished.
"You have some very garbled ideas about magical transformations," he remarked, "and if we didn't find natural items
better than transformed ones, magic-mongers would be
rich and you merchants would be poor." He handed Kara
the statuette.

"Aye," grumbled Ulrad. "Two halves of a walnut with
that chosen-brother of yours, that adventurer Valdart. Neither my trade wares nor my moneygems are good enough
for him this season, either."

"You must have tried to buy some memento he wants to
keep," said Torin.

"A little thing. A pendant with one of those glittery
orange stones they make on the other side of the western
ocean, set in blue metalwork like a pair of mer-birds with
their beaks touching and tails intertwined."

Kara glanced at Ulrad, her left eyebrow slightly raised.
"I've heard of such craftwork. On a bluemetal chain to
match the setting?"

Ulrad nodded. "And cheap enough, they say, if you can
cross the ocean to get them. I've heard they're worth no
more in the cities of that coast than a citron's worth in
Weltergrise, where they're grown."

"So cheap," said Kara. Ulrad reddened, as if just realizing he had blabbed matters more prudently left unsaid. In-
telligent crafters understood that traveling merchants
earned their livelihood through buying products where they
were worth less because of the growing climate, cheapness
of local materials, or certain crafting secrets, and selling
them where they were worth more because of their rarity.
But it was less than polite to discuss the principle while
doing business.

"Toycrafter!"

Torin looked up to see a thin figure in a light purple
robe—Iris the apprentice skyreader. She sprinted to his
booth, pushed in between the merchants, and repeated:
"Toycrafter!"

Ulrad started to say something, but Kara touched his arm behind the newcomer's back.

Usually Iris played her scholar's status and called Torin "son" although he was thirteen years older than she. He had always refused to reciprocate with "mother." This time she did not wait for him to say "Skyreader," but caught her breath and went on, "Talmar. Trouble with his breath. Collapsed in a fit. Scholars' Tent."

"Go," said Kara, "I'll watch your booth."

"Here!" Ulrad gestured at his selections. "At least let me pay for this pile before—"

"Let him go," said Kara. "It's a birth relation."

"My brother." Torin glanced at his toys. Not to trust Kara's offer would be rude, but this was only the third time he had seen her in ten years, only the fifth time he had seen Ulrad.

"But you can't heal him yourself, can you?" Ulrad grumbled. "You're not in that trade. You might as well—"

"My parents' younger child." The toymaker turned to Iris. "I know the way, Mother Skyreader. You can follow when you will."

Despite the situation, Iris grinned as she rooted her elbows on one end of the showledge.

Between living in the same neighborhood with her, tacitly committing his booth to her before witnesses, and bribing her with the term of address she had tried to tease out of him unsuccessfully for years, he thought he could trust her guardianship. Except, he remembered halfway across the fairground, she would turn independent skyreader next spring and likely leave this area. He would take a careful inventory of his possessions as soon as he got back.

The protective charm hung loose on its cord at the Scholars' Tent, but the brown silk doorcurtain was stiff. Torin put his palm on it and its folds melted into suppleness. He was grateful the magic-mongers had cast a selective spell; he would have disliked calling his way inside.

He pushed through, feeling the curtain start to stiffen again as it swished into place behind him.

Ugly sounds were coming from Talmar. They had put him in a cushioned, slantback chair at the east end of the tent, where he alternately hunched forward choking and lay back wheezing. Vague familiarity mixed with Torin's fear.

"Ah!" said the old sorceress Vathilda.

"Torin, oh, thank Cel!" Sharys jumped up from beside Talmar's chair and hurried around the table, her hand extended.

Torin took it and returned with her, each half-pulling the other. Talmar's face was swollen and purplish beneath a red rash, his eyelids puffed almost shut. He heaved up again into Vathilda's arms, coughed rackingly into a rag she held to his face, then fell back once more. Hilshar, who stood behind the chair, patted a compress over his forehead and cheeks.

Reaching the chair, Torin crouched on one knee beside it, loosed the young woman's hand from his and got hold of his brother's. They would probably never have chosen each other for friends. Their birth bond had usually lacked surface affection, but that mattered nothing now. "Talmarak," Torin called, then repeated it with yet another honorary syllable, "Talmarviak!"

"Aye." Old Vathilda discarded the used rag for a clean one. "But what's his sickness? Tell us that, Toymaker, and we may save his breath yet."

Torin shrugged helplessly.

"It started a few moments ago," said Sharys, "over nuts and brandy. Oh, Uncle Talmarak!" She knelt and groped for the wizard's other hand.

Torin glanced at the feast table, caught sight of the sky-reader and the judge.

"He was demonstrating a new trick with his globe," said Vathilda.

Torin saw the globe now, partly blocked from his sight by crystal bowls of nuts and crisps. The purple-robed sky-reader Laderan sat staring into it, prodding it with one

finger. Judge Alrathe moved quietly along the other end of
the table, sniffing the foods and drinks.

"He boasted it would earn him the third syllable to his
name," Vathilda went on, "or promotion to the silver robe,
or both."

Talmar tried to speak but instead heaved up again, pulling his hand from that of Sharys, and hacked into Vathilda's rag.

"So that's livecopper madness." Laderan gave the globe
another gingerly prod.

"If it is that," said Alrathe.

Talmar shook his head, fell back, and croaked, "I'm
sane." He felt for the young conjurer's hand again.

"And I don't call it a matter of simple power exhaus-
tion," said Vathilda. "You grew up beside him, Toymaker.
Did he ever fall to the boasting sickness, the Choking
Glory? Or daydreams and nightmares dropping into his
lungs?"

Torin shook his head, searching his memory. Daily life
with his brother had ended twenty years ago, when Torin
left home at the late prentice age of fifteen while Talmar
stayed to learn the family calling from their father.

"It resembles lung congestion," Alrathe suggested.

Vathilda's daughter Hilshar spoke for the first time.
"But why now, when not during the dust seasons?"

"Yes!" said Torin. "Once, the night of his First Name-
Lengthening—very much like this."

"No! Not—" The force of Talmar's protest brought on
another fit of choking.

Torin pressed his hand. "But not so severe."

"And it passed?" said Sharys.

"Of itself, or with healing?" said Vathilda.

Again Torin shrugged. "No . . . It might not have been
the same thing." He thought he lied. The event, being less
than pleasant to himself, had been stubborn in returning to
his memory, but now he felt sure Talmar's fit then had been
very similar. He also guessed the reason for Talmar's de-
nial: First Name-Lengthening, pride in new apprenticeship,

the boasting sickness. Already Vathilda's expression showed confidence that she was right. And when people suffered the Choking Glory, their comrades humbled instead of honoring them, for the sake of their health. Talmar *was* proud—too proud to confess the fatal weakness. Torin's own lungs felt divided—perhaps he increased the danger in trying to help disguise Talmar's pride, but perhaps, also, Talmar would prefer this death to the choking of his ambition. Besides, as nearly as Torin could recall, their mother had concentrated on mind-calming techniques that night. "Both our parents were there," he went on. "Father a high wizard and Mother a mage."

Talmar squeezed Torin's fingers and choked out, "My globe!"

"Forget your globe," said Vathilda. "Remember Irvathel's poem: 'Each of us is less than the lightest flake of paper ash.' Rest in—"

"My globe!" cried Talmar, and fell forward coughing more harshly than ever, dropping both Torin's hand and that of Sharys.

Torin rubbed his brother's back. "What is your new technique?" Flattery might soothe better than poetry.

Vathilda shrugged. "A toy to please young conjurers."

"It's not!" said Sharys. "It's a wonderful achievement, Uncle Talmarviak! He's invented a way of seeing the past," she explained to the toymaker.

"Only so much as the globe itself was there to see," said Vathilda.

"My globe!" Talmar insisted again.

"Brother Skyreader," said Vathilda with a sigh, "bring his globe."

Laderan brought it. Talmar sat back shakily, took the globe into his lap and, steadying it with his left fingers, caught Torin's hand and began moving it over the curved glass.

The toymaker tried to pull away. Talmar squeezed tighter, choked, closed his eyes and choked again. The veins in his forehead bulged, making his face even more painful to look at. Torin felt the mind-message tapping at his brain, punctuated by spasms: "Our family trade. Fifteen generations of magic-mongers. You the last—"

"No!" Torin jerked his hand from Talmar's grasp and shut his mind to the message. At once he regretted the reflex. Why not soothe his brother for once with a false promise? Keeping his brain closed to further mental messages, he put his hand back in Talmar's. "All right, brother, stop straining yourself. I'll . . . consider it. Teach me the new gesture."

With something between a wheeze and a hard sigh, Talmar guided his older brother's hand in an intricate finger work. When he lifted their hands away, the reflected images came to a standstill in the globe and then began to move in reverse. Distorted fingers and palm remained large, repeating the gestures from finish to start, lifted away to show Torin's brief refusal to learn the technique, returned momentarily for that abortive first start. The reflection of Laderan's hands came back as if covering the globe, and though in fact it lay unfingered in Talmar's lap, in imagery it seemed to be back in the skyreader's grasp.

Torin became aware that Sharys, Hilshar, Laderan, and even old Vathilda for all her show of scorn were watching with equal fascination. So, he sensed, was Judge Alrathe, who had come up behind him. Talmar started to sigh as in triumph, coughed again and covered his own mouth to choke the fit.

The image of Laderan's hands lifted away, and now the globe showed the view it would have reflected as it sat on the table a few moments ago, with the people moving backward.

"Marvellous!" Torin assured his brother. Talmar had dreamed since childhood of accomplishing something like this. "So you've done it at last! Wonderful."

"Oh, aye," said Vathilda.

Talmar bent forward in another ugly seizure.

"And much good it'll do him," Vathilda went on, "if he dies before presenting this for another syllable and a higher

rank. Toys, all toys." Holding the rags to his mouth, she
motioned for Hilshar to massage his back.

Even in his throes, Talmar was trying to press the globe
into his brother's hands.

"You're not dead yet," Torin was telling him over and
over, pushing the globe back to him. "You'll recover again.
This is passing, you're far from ripe for harvest."

Talmar gulped enough breath to choke out, "Elm!" He
had never changed his boyhood choice of tree to grow from
his grave.

"Yes, elm, eventually," Torin agreed, "but not for years.
You'll probably plant mine first."

"Here!" said Vathilda. "Take his precious globe before it
rolls away and smashes."

"I'll take it." Glad of the excuse, Torin slipped his
hands round the globe, stood, and crossed the little stream
over which they had positioned the tent.

As he reached the table, the doorcurtain softened and
swept back. Iris came into the tent, with Ulrad close behind.

"I have rightful business," said Ulrad. "Ah, there you
are, Toymaker."

Torin set the globe down with exaggerated care.
"Brother Merchant," he said, ashamed to think or ask, with
Talmar between breath and harvest, who was left watching
his own booth.

Ulrad started to hoist a filled bag, paused, and flushed,
looking toward the sick man. Torin followed his glance and
saw Talmar's eyes closed and forehead veins bulging.

"Aye, yes," said the merchant. "Well, let it wait,
Brother Toymaker." He had to speak above Talmar's
coughs. "I'll bring the payment along to you this evening,
tomorrow morning at latest." He began to back out,
glanced around, and said, "Yes, this evening then. Uh, the
curtain?"

"It is only stiff to keep unwanted people from coming
in," said Vathilda.

Ulrad touched the curtain, it softened at once, and he

hurried through. The sounds of Talmar's labors for breath filled the tent.

Torin realized that Iris was telling him something he felt anxious to hear. "What?" he asked.

"That storyteller happened to come by—Dilys. She said she'd watch your things until you came back."

Torin nodded. "I should go back long enough to move everything inside my tent, tie it up . . ."

"I'll go," said Hilshar. "Where do you keep your charm when it's not across your door?"

"Around my moneybox."

Torin took Hilshar's place behind the chair, she passed him the moistened compress and left the tent. He could trust Dilys; though he did not like the way she had let Ulrad and probably Kara walk off with their chosen purchases on trust, yet there were witnesses and Ulrad had already made one attempt to pay. He could also trust Hilshar, both as a neighbor and as a magician. Any student of magic above conjurer's rank could tie and untie a charm against thievery as well as its owner. Such skill required trustworthiness, so a magic-monger who stole was subject not only to judge's discipline but also to that of the Elder Mage. Magic-mongers might try to cheat openly, but even the most impoverished seldom risked stealing.

A few moments afterward, as Torin stroked his brother's forehead with the cool cloth, he realized that by giving him a healer's task, no matter how simple, Hilshar might have been working with Talmar's desire to transform the craftsman back into a student of magic.

Torin shook his head slightly. It would not hold, Talmar, he thought—though without attempting a mind-message. Fifteen generations of magic-mongers or not, I was born a toymaker.

He looked at the table. Many of the bowls, goblets, bottles, and plates had turned back to wood and clay, and the cloth was returning from silk to frayed linen, beginning with its silverlace edge. Usually the tableware stayed luxurious all day, sometimes two days without recasting the

spell. At a time like this, when so much energy was spent
elsewhere and so much concern filled the atmosphere, the
first or second jar could shiver an unused, ignored item
back into its true form. Even some of the delicacies had
changed back—citrons to small potatoes, dewmelons to
cabbages—and food transformations were generally more
stable. One theory was that the longer anything had been
harvested, the less permanently it would take transformation, but there were enough exceptions that the opposite
had been argued. Another theory proposed that the more
time and energy spent casting the transformation, the
longer it would last. The opposite of that had also been
suggested, perhaps in joke though it sometimes did seem to
hold true, as Torin had experienced with some of his own
accidental spells. The more study this area received, the
narrower its generalities appeared. The practical results
were that while magic-mongers could live in seeming lux-
ury despite actual poverty, their transformations were almost never permanent. The terms of impermanence tended
to be unpredictable and subject to infinite variables, so they
could rarely earn honest money selling the fruits of this
power, and even the magic-mongers themselves preferred
real to transformed items. Which was as well for the crafting classes.

Judge Alrathe sat in Laderan's old place, nibbling rare
whitenuts as they turned back into parched corn, and
watching Talmar's globe very intently.

Two

AT THIRTY-FIVE years old, one did not often find oneself Senior Storycrafter at any fair larger than thirty-five tents. Amberleaf Fair had forty-nine tents, not counting the animal shelters. Dilys liked to suspect that some of her mentors had made their excuses of minor illness, distance, or desire for rest in order to give her this experience.

She relished it all: choosing a pavilion site at the edge of the grounds, hanging lanterns in the forest to create an artistic play of shadows on the cloth walls, scheduling those adventurers who wanted to sell their tales between herself, Brinda, and Kivin. Four of the adventurers were older than Dilys, and Torin's friend Valdart was the same age, and that made her job even more enjoyable. Settled storycrafters always held authority over wanderers, who told tales only as a byproduct of their travels.

She delighted in overcoming the temptation to schedule everyone else so as to make herself seem a single bright aster in a garland of small leaves, culling the pattern instead to make each teller appear a blossom, set off or com-

plemented by predecessor, follower, and hour of day. She
was not so adept as her teacher Belvador at this arranging,
but she was not ill pleased with her results. Long tradition
gave the choice evening hours to the Senior Storycrafter, so
she could take them with an easy mind. She had stepped
onto the platform at twilight five times before now in her
life, but two of those occasions were when the Senior fell
sick unexpectedly and the other three were at gatherings so
small a platform seemed pretentious. At all other fairs and
festivals she had told her tales by daylight or midnight.

There were a few spots of of mildew on her first full day
of glory. But she had known since early last spring that
Torin thought he loved old Vathilda's granddaughter. Dilys
believed it a mistake, but she had adjusted well enough that
she felt capable of leaving them—Torin, Sharys, and now
Valdart—to disentangle their own problem. If she hoped
Sharys would persist in choosing Valdart, and blushed for
that hope—because her objective reaction was that the adventurer would make Sharys a worse chosen than the toymaker—at least she could keep her opinions secret.

She had had less time to assimilate High Wizard Talmar's sickness. But Torin's brother was important to her
only as Torin's brother and a fellow creature. The lack of
amiable qualities Talmar had shown her over the years had
kept them polite acquaintances, careful to stay outside the
exhalations of each other's lungs. As nearly as she could
observe, the wizard was even less amiable to his sibling.
Perhaps because Dilys could not like Talmar, she found it
difficult to believe his danger was mortal. The first rumors
had inspired her to stroll past Torin's booth again. Iris
called the situation grave, but the apprentice skyreader
liked to puff every little excitement. Hilshar had spoken
with much greater optimism. True, Hilshar had come to tie
all Torin's things behind his charm against thievery, which
errand implied that the wizard was sick enough to cost his
brother half a day of fair business. Nevertheless, the storycrafter preferred to believe that a magician, with the magic-
monger's insight into healing, gave a more trustworthy

statement than an excitable young skyreader.

So Dilys used Talmar's complaint as an exercise to drain her attention from her own platform nervousness, and hoped the toymaker would still be able to come and hear her. Returning from his booth, she stopped at the story pavilion and listened with keen satisfaction to part of Kivin's performance, then slipped to her own tent, ate a small supper, washed her mouth and upper body and changed her tunic. Bright embroidery helped stir interest in the storytelling as you walked about the fair, but simple duskwhite was better when you sat on the platform telling your tales, framed by the sides of the old carved darkwood chair and the shadows of trees with their last autumn leaves falling on the tentcloth behind you. Give your audience just enough to look at without distracting them from what they heard. She went back gently to the pavilion.

Torin had not come for her tales.

She could not have failed to see him. The adventurer Rondak had preceded her. All but two of his listeners remained, and Kivin's young sister Kip collected the money-gems they gave to hear the next teller, while almost thirty more came, paying at the entrance, as Dilys trailed out her bait-tale. In all, she gathered seventy-three, an excellent-sized audience, more than half the people present at this Amberleaf Fair, but not so large that a dearly familiar face could blend into anonymity. Her listeners had ample room to spread their cushions, and even in the muted dusk she had a good overview from the platform.

Folding away her disappointment, she began the time-venerated saga of Ilfting the Dwarf. But she decided to omit her own tale of how he rescued one of Thyrna's brightwings. She had first tried that tale on the toymaker in a private storytelling the first year of their acquaintance, so by leaving it out tonight she in some way both paid Torin for not coming and saved it for him in case he came on the middle or last day of the fair. Fortunately, Ilfting tales both old and new were so many that a cycle could be tailored to any length around the three basic events of his birth, his climbing the Teln-tree, and his death.

By her listeners' silence, their upturned faces and the way they shifted position only between episodes, she knew she had succeeded in hiding her own hurt, and by the time Ilfting neared Teln-top she herself was unaware of any events in her personal life. Dusk became full dark, limned by lantern-cast shadows on tent walls and pricked by the candles that flanked storyteller's chair and listeners' entrance. Her audience swelled from tale to tale as more fairgoers chose to enter the carpeted area, Brinda lowering the payment to fit the length of time that remained. The autumn moon, nearly half full, rose high enough to lend its glow to pavilion walls and roof.

Dilys was beginning the last tale when Torin came after all. She saw his honey-brown hair as he bent over Brinda's table to learn the adjusted price, his brown hand as he rolled a carved stone into the cloth-lined box. So careful with his moneygems, he nevertheless paid for cushion space when only the end tale of her performance remained.

She did not break the narrative flow, but she fitted in the episode of the brightwing's rescue, putting it into Thyrna's greeting when the spirit came to harvest the dwarf. It worked very smoothly.

"So Ilfting died with his eyes closed," she ended, "and a great goldentree grew from his grave. Thyrna's brightwings played among its branches for many generations."

She rose and bowed. Now that her performance was done and the audience singing an enthusiastic song of applause, she directed one slight, uncraftish nod at the toymaker before descending and leaving through the tellers' door behind the platform.

Valdart stood outside tapping his fingertips on the sides of his folded arms. As she emerged, he started in.

She held him back. "When they finish singing for me, adventurer. I've told you before, remember the pauses. You'll have plenty of time while they're settling down again and paying to hear you."

He shrugged and began snapping his knuckles. She

would have been as well pleased to allow him inside early so that she could enjoy both her sons and her wait in solitude, still, she doubted that Torin would leave the audience before the end of the applause.

But they gave her a second song—rare distinction even for a Senior Storycrafter—and while they were still singing this, the toymaker came around the pavilion.

He looked at his old friend the adventurer. Valdart looked down, snapped two knuckles over again, looked up once more and met Torin's gaze with a small grin. Dilys was glad the lanterns hung so high that their three human shadows hovered short on the tentcloth, hidden by the platform from the people inside.

Torin smiled awkwardly and touched the adventurer's arm. "Good tale-crafting, Valdartak."

Valdart returned the shoulder clap and ducked inside. Dilys closed her lips against any comment that might hover too near the situation between these two men and the young conjurer. Instead, she moved at a slant into the edge of the forest, Torin following.

A little away from the pavilion and safely private from the dangers of casting shadows on its cloth or being overheard, she leaned against a thick oak. "You missed most of my best tales, Toymaker," she began in a teasing tone.

"I've heard most of them before. But that was a nice touch you added tonight, about the brightwings in Ilfting's goldentree."

"You could make it into a new toy." The sudden idea enthused her. "Ilfting's grave—a carved hill, perhaps—with a shaft and a little trapdoor. A little figure of Ilfting to slip into the shaft, and a goldentree to fit into the top of the trapdoor when it's closed. And a few little brightwings, of course, to move in and out of the branches. With movable wings, maybe."

"Maybe . . . someday, not yet."

She remembered his brother's sickness, and the proposed toy seemed out of place. "Torin, how serious is it?"

"He's made us leave him alone for the night."

Alone—to wait for Thyrna in her role as Harvester of
Life. The storycrafter took the toymaker's right hand in
both her own. "Torinel."

"I wonder," he said, "if magic and toymaking might be
combined. If that toy goldentree might drop its own leaves
and keep growing new ones, if the little brightwings flew
by themselves—"

"Torin, no!"

"You're right. The judges would never allow it. Unfair
to honest toymakers."

"He's been trying to change you again, hasn't he?" Her
voice quivered.

"We can't be angry, not this time. Think—he sees our
family's tradition dying with him, perhaps tonight."

She could be angry with High Wizard Talmar, using his
weakness to weaken his brother, but she bit back the worst
of her annoyance. "Torinel, no. You're a crafter. Start your
own tradition. Your parents had other prentices."

"Only three, and none of them birth relations."

"Nevertheless. And wherever she is now, your mother
probably has another prentice travelling with her. That's
enough to keep your family's own style alive, and if it's
not, better to let something die in its own time than force it
to stay alive when it's already returning to its earth." She
pressed his right hand closer. "You've climbed too long
and too high."

"But if I've been climbing the wrong mountain?"

"There is no wrong mountain, Toymaker."

He put his left hand on hers so that all of their fingers
touched. "Storycrafter, thanks," he said. But his shoulders
still slumped, and as he disengaged his hands and turned
away, she wondered how far anyone could help another.

As far, it should be, as anyone could hinder another.

But perhaps the influence of a dying birth sib would
inevitably prove stronger than that of a mere friend. The
friend aimed for the fellow creature's individual welfare,
but the sibling aimed for the welfare of the family. A family was larger than an individual and older than a friend-

ship. This particular friendship had lasted only ten years, less than a third of either party's lifetime.

Valdart had been Torin's friend for more than two thirds of their lifetimes. His counsel might carry more weight, and he might feel all the readier to give it since Sharys would be more likely to choose Torin the fellow magic-monger than Torin the toymaker.

But Sharys would probably add her influence to Talmar's. So might her mother and grandmother—magic-mongers all, and magic-mongers seemed of all students the most eager to swell their numbers in disregard of material poverty. Dilys could not send for Torin's gnarly old teacher Yarkon: he had met Thyrna last spring. Torin's mother, Mage Talysidor, might counsel her son to climb his own trail, as she had when he was a boy; but after her husband's death her journeys had grown longer, farther, and more secret. Thus, Talmar could claim the strength of all the dead or absent family. Added to the strength of his own dying, it gave him great power.

"Oh, Torin," the storycrafter whispered in the direction he had disappeared. "Climb your own mountain, breathe your own air!"

She slipped back into the pavilion and sat hidden behind the platform, trying to hear Valdart's storytelling with de- tached interest. He was not bad. Though his tales depended more on substance than style, the substance was sufficient and the roughness did not detract, might even enhance the matter, as if he were sitting at your table telling you his adventures conversationally. It had an unpolished charm which she half feared marring were he to adopt the sugges- tions she could offer.

When he descended, she drew him outside. "You de- serve that song, adventurer," she murmured as they stood listening.

His broad chest swelled, shoulders lifting to make more room for lungs. He displayed his teeth in a full grin and rubbed his strong brown hand over his golden hair. "No suggestions, Senior Crafter?"

His consciousness of his own perfection dissipated the friendly feeling she had just nurtured. Beckoning him to the fringe of woods, she felt much tempted to give him those suggestions, lesson him in how to improve his style. By the time they were far enough from the pavilion to talk easily, however, she had softened herself again. If she tried to instruct him in her present mood, it would be too much like a word-whipping, and for Torin's sake she needed Valdart's goodwill.

"Well, Master Storycrafter?" he said, putting hands on hips as he lounged against a tree.

She lounged against another and folded her arms. "How well do you know High Wizard Talmar?"

He shrugged. "Used to tag after us sometimes when we were all saplings, until he lengthened his name and decided he was climbing for higher peaks. Why?"

"This afternoon's rumors seem to have been well based."

"Oh." He had clearly forgotten them in the flux of his performance. She could hardly blame him for that, when she had done the same.

"Dead?" he went on.

"They left him alone to wait for Thyrna. That was Torin's news."

"Oh. Well. Taggish Tal. . . . Some of them were calling it livecopper madness?"

"Maybe." Torin had not said and Dilys had failed to ask. She was always failing to ask the obvious. "Livecopper madness would be the kindest explanation. He's been trying to transform Torin back into a magic-monger."

Valdart did not miss a breath. "Well, maybe our Torinel always was more magic-monger than toymaker. What rank would he pick up? Magician or even sorcerer, I'd guess."

"He's crafted for twenty years!" She included his apprenticeship.

"I've adventured for twenty years, and I'm thinking it's ripe time to change callings."

"Oh?" said Dilys.

"I've seen enough to make a good shopcrafter, or even plant a farm."

"And of course Sharys would prefer a farmcrafter to a fellow magic-monger."

Valdart pushed away from his tree. "Aye, Senior Story-crafter, maybe she would. Still a conjurer herself at nine-teen—maybe she'd rather raise her children with a crafter than with a fellow student who could have graduated to magician by his fourteenth summer."

"Valdartak!" said Dilys a little desperately, catching his arm. "Whatever you think—shouldn't people choose their own trails? If some sibling told you you had to settle down now in some shop or farm, or else told you you had to go on adventuring . . . ?"

"Aye," he admitted. "True enough."

"Adventurer . . . Valdartak, Torin needs friends tonight. Will you go to him?"

Valdart shook off her hand. "No, I don't think I will. He came to you with his news. He didn't wait for me. It's fairly clear he wants to be alone now."

This time she let the adventurer stride away. She turned and fingered the bark of the silvertree she had leaned on, trying to sense, as Torin could, the life that was tucking into its winter trance. The air that came out of her lungs felt as cold as when they drew it in. "Yes, perhaps he does want to be alone tonight," she whispered. "Alone, like his brother. Alone to wait for his own death as toymaker."

Three

JUDGE ALRATHE ALSO sat alone that night, pondering.

It was a pity, though understandable, that the high wizard had insisted his globe be carried back with him to his own tent. An old and favorite tool, especially one for which its owner had devised a marvellous new use, must make the best of all deathbed toys. At least, so Alrathe supposed; judges might have individual talismans to help focus their thoughts—a gem, a ring of braided hair, a small toy—but no tool connected of its own nature with their work, so they could only guess at the strength of attachment that grew between magic-mongers, skyreaders, or crafters and the tools of their study or craft. Alrathe had even avoided a thought-focusing toy, preferring a candle flame, or the play of colors and darkness behind closed eyelids.

Nevertheless, the judge would have liked to study that backward-unfolding view of the past afternoon once again. If the toymaker had learned the technique, so might a judge. Torin, or course, was part magic-monger thanks to his family and childhood, but Alrathe was a student, and at least two poets had written that one mark of a good student was versatility. Moreover, it seemed that the globe began its backview from the moment of the gesture, so every hour that went by increased the time one would have to wait for today's feast sequence. Talmar might have some additional trick for adjusting the time element, but he had not shown it to his brother, and it risked dying with him tonight.

If Talmar died, the problem would become unimportant in his own case, and the likelihood was low that many other cases in future would hinge on what a globe could review. Magic globes were not common outside the homes of magic-mongers. Not all magickers were eager to sell them, and most crafters preferred working by natural light.

Even as Alrathe's mind digressed to the usefulness or non-essentiality of magic globelight—or so it seemed, though a doze might have intervened—a sudden gleam lit up the crimson tent from outside. It struck the cloth wall facing Talmar's tent, and seemed to have the quality of double-filtered light, but it faded almost at once. Perhaps it marked the wizard's harvesting. Or perhaps he had simply illuminated his globe in a moment of delirium.

Alrathe sighed. Talmar's disease was a case not for judges but for healers. And the eldest healer seemed satisfied it was Choking Glory. To Alrathe, it seemed like simple sensitivity, but Vathilda had not appeared receptive to the suggestion of a judge in versatile mood. Vathilda was not only experienced in her skill, she was treating a fellow magic-monger. And old rumor said that in early youth she herself had stumbled on the Choking Glory; that was why she had never graduated to higher rank than sorceress nor added any syllable beyond the third to her name.

Unlike livecopper madness, which endangered no one except careless magic-mongers, Choking Glory also affected judges and skyreaders, sometimes even crafters and adventurers. In the most painstaking self-examination Alrathe remained an ignorant innocent, unable to remember any personal soul-stubbings on pride, only a few vanities hard to distinguish from desire for neat cleanliness. Still, why should Talmar have fallen to Choking Glory only at First Name-Lengthening and today? He had apparently shown no such symptoms at his graduations to magician, sorcerer, wizard, and then high wizard before the age of thirty-two, the youngest magic-monger of his generation to wear dark azure.

Torin found that Hilshar had not only tied his charm across his doorcurtain, she had stiffened the curtain itself. That was unnecessary. It was also suggestive. Magic-mongers stiffened their tent doors to show they did not wish to be disturbed. Other people tied the cords outside the curtain.

Besides, it seemed futile. Whereas the general spell on the Scholars' Tent made the cloth stiffen again each time, the specific one on the toymaker's door would dissolve at his touch and not renew unless he renewed it.

Or unless he was already, in his hidden soul, more student than crafter. Once enspelled, magic-mongers' private doorcurtains responded to their owners' secret wishes. Sometimes magickers in the beginning ranks, conjurers and magicians and occasionally the younger sorcerers, did not realize their own desire for privacy until they saw their curtains grow stiff. Torin touched his curtain, untied the charm, entered, retied the charm across the doorway and let the cloth swing back into place.

Was it stiffening again? Not enough moonlight penetrated the tent for him to see clearly, nor could he tell by feeling, for his touch would redissolve the spell instantly.

He considered his own small magic globe, a First Name-Lengthening gift that he had kept all these years for its light. But this evening he hesitated to use it, and lit a candle instead. Its flickering glow showed his doorcurtain hanging pliable to the drafts. He clung to the reassurance, but wondered whether his globe would have shown the same result.

He shivered. The day's fragile autumn warmth had dis-

solved with the sun. He had taken off his short festival
cape about midday and not caught it up when they called
him to his brother's side. His long cloak was in his travelling chest, and Dilys had set his showledge on top of the
chest. He looked around and saw that she had left his short
cape folded on his bed, where it made a patch of lighter
brown. He went and put it on, then peeled up the top blanket and swung it round his shoulders for an overcloak.
Half-thinking, he tucked the sheets and lower blanket back
into place around the mattress, stuffed yesterday with dry
leaves and pinefeathers from the woods around the fairground. He remembered yesterday's work wistfully.

Feeling too tired to carry his brazier outside, kindle it
and wait for the flames to sink into slow emberfire, he
knelt beside his chest. His long cloak and both blankets
should keep him warm enough for the night. But he had to
lift the showledge down, and it was still laden with toys.
He needed a few moments' rest. He found space between a
group of cake trinkets and a family of nested owls to put
the candle, warmed his fingers over its flame, sank from
kneeling to sitting, and gazed at the ledge.

Dilys had carried it inside very carefully, or else rearranged it after setting it on the chest. Each toy was upright
and in place. Perhaps not in the exact place he had origi-
nally displayed it, but he had left two merchants examining
his goods, and maybe other would-be buyers had come
while he was gone. He tried to make a mental list of what
Kara and Ulrad should pay him for tomorrow, by compar-
ing what remained with what he remembered setting out.
Eventually he noticed a piece of paper beneath the statuette
of Ilfting the Dwarf. After a moment he built enough energy to reach up, lift the statue, retrieve the paper, and find
that Dilys had left him a list of Kara's and Ulrad's selections. Not the prices, she could not have known those, but
concise descriptions, followed by a note that she had allowed no one except Ulrad and Kara to take anything away
from the ledge, but Merprinel the mirrorcrafter was interested in the necklace of spangles within latticework links

all carved from a single length of silverwood, and young Nar wanted the darkring top and one of the stone turtles.

The statuette of Ilfting nodded at Torin. "A good friend, that storycrafter."

Torin was refolding her list. "I'm sorry. I didn't mean to charm you."

"I suspect she'd like you for a chosen," Ilfting went on.

"She had long enough to say so."

"So did you, Son."

"Not so long," Torin objected. "Eighteen is very young to marry. My fingers must have slipped when I touched you."

"Aye, just as our Dilys was making up her mind this spring, you go flittering away around that young conjure rosebud."

"Shall I correct the mistake?" Torin lifted his hand. It shook with weariness and the fingernails looked dirty. So did the fingers and knuckles, when he squinted at them, as if they were covered with soot, and the skin below abnormally pale. It must be the candlelight. He reached towards Ilfting. "Shall I transform you back?"

"Not yet, Son." The statuette rapped Torin's fingertip with one tiny fist that stung like an insect. "Not with a claw in that condition."

The toymaker retracted his hand and gazed at a droplet of blood bulging up on the fingertip. "I must have left a splinter in you."

"Like enough. You're not the crafter you think you are, sapling."

"I shouldn't have carved you my old teacher's face." In fact, Torin did not think he had been conscious of intending the likeness.

"Carve with the grain, boy." The statuette rubbed its nose. "Let your wood do what it wants. You try to carve like some glory-choking magicker. Always did and always will."

"She's not glory-choking," said Torin, and frowned because something seemed wrong with his memory. For a

moment he had thought it was Sharys who was deathly
sick, and Talmar bending over her. No, Sharys and Valdart
were together somewhere, Valdart giving her his marriage
toy from a distant place, and Talmar was lying alone waiting for the Harvest Spirit. Torin looked around to see
whose tent he sat in.

"Aye," said Ilfting, "but toymaking's a richer study than
magic-mongering these years. You chose well enough
there, sapling, if comfort was your want."

"Talmar chose for glory."

"He chose for your family, that one."

"I suffered my hungry seasons."

Ilfting snorted. "Hungry! You with magic to keep your
belly full."

"You're wood yourself. Maybe you can eat sawdust. We
have to start with real food. We can't transform apples out
of sand—it changes back to sand inside."

"Maybe that's your brother's sickness."

"They're all magic students. They know better."

The dwarf began to clean his fingernails with the
splinter in his fist. "You're the one chose for glory. Carving
your precious name on every toy."

"Only the first letter. Only the flying bird."

"Your brother might've gone to skyreading if you hadn't
turned toycrafter first."

"No," Torin protested. "I was the only one in fifteen
generations. If he'd wanted to transform, too, who could
guess . . . ?"

"Or to judging. But not to crafting. Not Talmarak. Adventuring, maybe."

"I was cold and hungry for years. Even now my tent has
more patches than Talmar's has, beneath his spells."

"Because you're a miserly young sapling. You could
live soft as a townmerchant if you chose."

"It's not miserly to marry."

"You with your old globe, calling it for free light. Better
pinch out this candle, lad. You're burning moneygems.
Besides, much lower and it'll singe my cap."

"You're alive now. You can walk away."

Ilfting hammered his thighs with his fists and shrugged. "No feeling already. You're not that powerful by accident, conjurer."

The candle was burning down with a speed that suggested defective molding. Torin reached up to pinch the wick.

When next he became aware of his surroundings, the tent walls were gray with dawnlight. The candle, not so short as he seemed to remember it, had been pinched out and the wax was hard.

He took the statuette of Ilfting into his hands and turned it around and around, examining it for spatters of candlewax (he found none) and trying to determine if the posture was exactly as he had carved it. Speech was unusual in animated statues; sometimes, however, transformed toy animals did emit the approximations of barks, mews, and so on. He thought of attempting to bring the statuette to life on purpose and asking it whether last night's conversation had been waking or dreaming, but timidity quenched temptation. He rearranged the toys his arms had displaced in cradling his head, stood and stretched to unknot his muscles, lifted the showledge down at last, set it on the tent floor, rearranged the blanket-cloak around his shoulders, sat again and opened the chest.

Although his brother might be dead, reason told him to eat now. He had eaten no regular meal last night, only a boiled egg, some almond paste that was turning back into cheese, and a glass of wine from the scraps of the scholars' banquet. He was hungry, and his food supply was neat in the top case-ledge, but nothing looked appetizing. He picked up a boiled egg and debated transforming it into an apple or citron.

Ten years ago he had entered life as independent crafter with the firm resolution to go on avoiding any magic work —except globelight—as strictly as he had done throughout his apprenticeship. A winter of meals as monotonous as they were scanty and cheap had chipped away that resolu-

tion, until on the first Spring Quarter-season day he and
Dilys spent together in woods and meadow, he had used a
few transformations to vary the food in his basket. He had
quickly fallen into the habit of such indulgence. The more
secure he felt in his chosen craft, the less a minor magic
spell for his own and close friends' comfort had troubled
him; and it had not seemed to make accidental toy transformations any more frequent. Nevertheless, as he pros-
pered and persuaded himself to buy real delicacies, he had
been climbing farther and farther above transformed food.

Unfortunately, the real delicacies he had brought with
him consisted of a little pear cordial, some special herbs,
and a box of mushroom cheese with caper sauce—all either too heavy for his stomach just now, or requiring
freshly heated water. He rubbed his hands over the egg
again, felt stickiness, and discovered that without consciously deciding, he had transformed it into a honeyed
citron.

Three accidental transformations within two days was
abnormal. He hoped Ilfting had been a dream.

He doubted the citron's complete edibility, as he had not
peeled the egg. With how much comfort would a whole
eggshell digest as the citron took back its original substance inside him? He might have eaten it regardless, but
both logic and stiff weariness said this was no time to dabble in self-correction. He dropped the fruit back into the
tray, noticing its squish where an unpeeled egg would have
cracked, and looked around for a rag to wipe his hands.

He frowned for a moment at the dark bulge on his bed.
Hadn't he smoothed the lower blanket down last night after
pulling off the topmost for an overcloak? Then he saw that
the bulge was a carrying-bag . . . one he did not recognize.

Pulling the blanket tighter around him, he approached
the bed. The carrying-bag appeared full of a single rather
large ball or small melon. The dark cloth, threadbare and
frayed between its patches, rose smooth on top and fell into
a nest of casual creases round its base, the whole looking
all the stranger for its inanimate innocence.

He picked it up, found the cloth double-layered (a second bag slipped inside the first), and the ball within hard and slippery. He knelt and rolled it out upon the bed.

It was his brother's magic globe, reflecting Talmar's curve-distorted face. Torin's blanket slid from his back and he shivered a little, but did not retrieve it.

He could tell by the azure background, the color of high wizardry, that the globe reflected a scene in Talmar's own tent. The azure was bright. Torin located his brother's imaged tent door; it was open to show sunshine. Talmar looked healthy, though the review seemed to skip moments as the high wizard's hands loomed in with their practised gestures.

The toymaker had just picked it up for a closer examination when someone shouted "Tor!" outside his tent.

He started, his fingers instinctively tightening around the globe.

"Tor!" again. That was Valdart truncating his name so rudely.

Or urgently. He might bring news, and adventurers learned shorter manners. "I'm awake," Torin called in reply. "I'm coming." He replaced the globe on his bed and rose, stumbled on the cloak-blanket, gathered it up and, after a few heartbeats of half-consideration, dropped it over the globe.

When he straightened and turned, Valdart was entering the tent.

Some discourtesies could not go overlooked even from adventurers and old friends. "The cord was tied," said Torin.

"So was mine last night." The adventurer thrust his right hand forward and opened it, displaying a citron. "That didn't hold you outside, did it?"

Perhaps this was the dream. Last night's conversation with Ilfting had certainly been more coherent.

Valdart closed his fist around the citron again and shook it. "Well? Are you going to change it back?"

"Into what? When did I come to your tent last night?"

"Into my bluemetal pendant with the orange glitter-gem!" said Valdart, mixing in several extra and ugly adventurers' words.

"No one would transform jewelry into food."

"My marriage token for the little conjurer! Addle you, chosen brother, what kind of rotten trick..." Valdart's glance caught on the food ledge in Torin's open chest, where the honeyed citron was untransforming into an egg. "Practice?"

"I suppose one of us is dreaming." Torin stretched out his hand. "But I'll try to undo the transformation."

Valdart stepped close enough to lay the fruit on his friend's palm, but kept his own hold on one end, pinching the rind. Torin concentrated for a moment. The piece of fruit remained a piece of fruit. "It's a real citron, Valdartak."

"Will you change it back, or do I go to the judges?"

"It's not a transformation," Torin repeated. "It's a real citron."

Valdart snatched it from his hand. "Tightening up your work, hey? Addle you, Tor! The judges, then—or your fellow magickers. I understand they're pretty severe about breaking doorcharms against thieves."

He left. The curtain went on swinging for several moments. Torin looked at the egg that had briefly been a piece of fruit; its shell was cracked. He turned and looked at his bed; Talmar's globe was still there. He looked at the statuette of Ilfting; it grinned as widely as when it was first carved, and he envied it. He looked back at the doorway. The curtain had not yet stopped swinging.

He sighed. He ought to wait for the judges—one judge, Alrathe, the only one here—or Vathilda and Hilshar if Valdart really meant to summon them, but magic-mongers could have no authority over a toymaker. Surely neither judge nor senior magic students would think him irresponsible, however, if under the circumstances he went right away to learn his brother's condition, even after Valdart's warning of judgment.

The decision made, he went quickly, stopping just long enough to retie his charm and doorcords in a simple knot. Had his old friend intended thievery this morning, the charm would have kept him out. He could neither have untied it, slipped beneath the cord, nor slit the tent wall. But the protective magic had not been fitted to simple rudeness. And Torin had signalled that he would let the visitor in.

Two steps from his tent, he wondered if he should have brought Talmar's globe. He hesitated, then strode on without taking time to focus logic on the question.

More than two thirds of the fairgoers were already astir. The morning was cloudy and threatened rain, which inspired boothkeepers to seize every hour they could before having to display inside their tents or not at all. Young Scap and Eldan the adventurer stopped Torin to ask what news he had of his brother, the high wizard. Everyone else, seeing him hurrying alone to the scholars' part of the fairground, politely made way with sympathetic nods.

Valdart must have left a wake through them only moments ago, but no one commented on his passage. Apparently he had kept his complaint for a private thing between himself, Torin, and the judge. Old friendship still held that much power.

The skyreader Laderan was standing before Merprinel's showledge, looking over her mirrors. Torin paused, with some idea that the skyreader, as a student who had been at the scholars' banquet yesterday, might have reliable news. "Father," he asked, "how is Talmar?"

Laderan shrugged. "His curtain was still stiff when I went past half an hour ago. The young conjurer was waiting outside."

"Torin," said Merprinel, "Cel surround you."

"Thank you, Aunt." Torin hurried on. He had only a few hundred more paces and a turn around the corner of the Scholars' Pavilion to his brother's small azure tent.

No one stood outside, and the folds of the doorcurtain flowed with the draughts.

Judge Alrathe's crimson tent neighbored Talmar's at a comfortable distance for privacy. The judge's doorcurtain appeared to be swinging like Torin's after Valdart pushed through. The adventurer must be with the judge even now.

Heart catching between his lungs, Torin held Talmar's curtain aside and went in.

Sharys was kneeling beside the wizard's bed, her hand on his brow. His eyes were closed and he continued to work for each breath.

Torin approached.

Sharys glanced up at him. "He's asleep," she murmured. "Exhausted."

He knelt beside her and looked at the sick man. This sleep had soothed away very few traces of labor and pain. A sleep of desperation rather than relief. Nevertheless, Talmar was alive, and taking some kind of rest.

"His door softened only a few moments ago," Sharys went on. "He must have been awake and waiting for Thyrna until then. Maybe all night through."

Now that he was here, the toymaker could scarcely believe the truth of his brother's magic globe on his own bed. He looked around Talmar's tent, hoping to see it somewhere.

"What is it?" said Sharys.

"His globe."

"What? Oh." Softly, she examined the bedding and floor around it, then searched the small tent with her own gaze. "But he was so insistent last night. How ugly! For someone to come in and take it away from him now!" She stared into Torin's face. "They must have taken it from his very hands. But how could they?"

Not that being washed and groomed would have made the revelation easier, but suddenly Torin was aware of his beard stubble, the wrinkles in his tunic, the fact that he had not even pulled comb through hair. He turned his face a little away.

"Could he have softened his door for a while in the night?" Sharys said. "Maybe if he thought . . . or if his mind slipped—or, oh Cel! if he wanted help—and then for someone to take advantage of it to steal his globe!"

Torin breathed deeply and said, "It's in my tent."

"What?"

"I don't know how it came to be there. I woke up this morning and found it." He groped for her hand. "Sharilys, if he asks for it, I have it safe."

After half a breath, she said, "Then bring it back, why not?"

"I . . . Maybe you can come for it, or send someone. Your mother or grandmother. But I should keep to my tent. I should be waiting there now. Maybe later today . . ."

"Torin?" she said.

He realized he had to tell her the rest. Otherwise she would hear Valdart's version first. He was fortunate his old friend had not complained to her already. "Sharilys, whatever you hear, whatever Valdart thinks . . ."

"Yes?"

"The marriage toy he was planning to give you. It's gone. He thinks I transformed it into a piece of fruit. I didn't."

"Oh," she said. "Marriage toys." Talmar coughed in his sleep and she turned back to him.

"I didn't, Sharilys," the toymaker repeated. "I didn't leave my own tent—"

Talmar choked, hard, yet without waking up. "Brother Torin," said Sharys, "can't we talk about all that afterward? Where's the water? Here."

He helped her moisten a compress, arranged things within her reach, and left her stroking Talmar's head, enwrapped in the healer's concern that could crowd out all lesser problems, even choice of a lifelong mate.

Four

IT BEHOOVED THE only judge at a fair to remain available. Alrathe's doorcords had dangled loose all night. The judge was heating breakfast water when the adventurer burst in.

"Cousin?" said Alrathe, not remembering his name.

Having entered impetuously, the newcomer proceeded to stand near the door as if perplexed, opening his mouth and closing it again, fisting and unfisting one large brown hand while the other stayed clenched.

Alrathe smiled. "I am one of those who prefers 'Cousin' to any other term of address."

The adventurer nodded. "Well . . . uh, Cousin Judge, it's a robbery . . ."

"They are too common nowadays. Have you any idea who the thief might be?"

"Aye." The adventurer flushed. "Well, not a robbery, exactly, but it might as well have been. There! Look at this." He unclenched his hand to display an orange citron of the thumb-sized variety.

"A trade to which you had not agreed?"

41

"A transformation! Uh . . . Cousin, last night this was a bluemetal and orangestone pendant from beyond the western ocean."

"Transformation?" Alrathe took the fruit, pinched it gently, sniffed it. It seemed genuine: fragrant, slightly yielding within its somewhat hardened rind, filled with promise of succulence. But transformations were the study of magic-mongers, not judges. "Only four among the fairgoers could have effected a transformation," said Alrathe. "One of them has lain near death since yesterday afternoon, and the other three are members of a single family. It may prove difficult to confirm the fact of transformation."

"Your counting's wrong," said the adventurer. "That is . . . asking your pardon, Cousin Judge, but there's a fifth person here who does transformations, and he's the one did this."

Alrathe gazed at the complainant. "Do you mean Talmar's brother Torin, the toycrafter?"

The complainant bent his golden head and studied the threadbare floor rugs. "Aye, Torin. And I've known him since we were one-syllable saplings, Cousin Judge."

The small kettle on Alrathe's brazier entered the conversation with the rattle that preceded full boil.

"I have three blends," said the judge. "Sweet, savory, and plain." While the adventurer hesitated as if unsure that judges offered refreshment to clients, Alrathe added, "All are of common, local herbs, nothing rare or exotic."

"Savory," said the adventurer. "With thanks, Cousin Judge."

"Alrathe." The judge got two cups, put them and the citron on top of the closed travelling chest, added savory herbs to one cup and sweet to the other. "And your name —I was about to ask when my kettle interrupted—Valdin?"

"Valdart."

"Cousin Valdart." Alrathe poured the boiling water, took the cup of sweetblend, and sat on the bed.

With a glance at the citron, Valdart took the cup of savory and sat cross-legged on the rugs.

In general, Alrathe thought reluctant complainers preferable to those who gushed out their stories. If a judge did sometimes wonder why the reluctant ones had come at all, often their wrongs could be dissolved in an hour, without bringing in the person complained against. And reluctance was more lovable than eagerness, particularly in a case of old friends. But it did demand craftwork from the judge. "You were one of last night's adventurer storytellers?" Alrathe inquired.

"Aye. You didn't come to hear us, Cousin?"

"I regret not." Listening to stories well told was among Alrathe's greatest pleasures, but yesterday evening had been spent pondering the malady of the wizard who lay next door. "One boast of adventurers' tales is their truth."

"That mine are." The adventurer grinned. "Well, mostly. Maybe a few decorations here and there. But good ones. The Senior Storycrafter herself admitted I earned my song of applause."

Alrathe nodded. "Good! Now leave out any decorations, but otherwise tell me the tale of your orangestone pendant as you tell an audience your adventures."

Valdart cleared his throat, drank a few swallows of herbwater, and cleared his throat again. "Well, Cousin. There's the little conjurer, Mother Vathilda's granddaughter, pretty Sharilys. When I came home to my old places this year and found her almost grown . . . Well, you've seen how things grow between chosen and chosen. So I had one fine orangestone and bluemetal neck pendant left from my last trip across the western ocean, one I'd been saving for a special use, and night before last I offered it to little Sharilys for a marriage-bed token. She didn't take it right away, but she promised me my answer in the morning. Well, next morning—yesterday morning—she told me she'd just talked to my old chosen brother Torin and promised him she'd wait until the last night of this fair before she took my token." Valdart worked his jaw for a moment and turned the cup in his hands. "Old Vathilda and her family, they're neighbors of his, and it seems Torin's grown a lik-

ing for Sharys himself that way. Had his own marriage toy
that he tried to give her, one of his own crafting. Might
make even bluemetal and orangestone from beyond the
ocean look like cheap craftwork. So. Well, I thought he'd
come to me yesterday, talk it through face to face. He
didn't, Cousin. The next I saw him, he'd come to the Storytellers' Pavilion that night while the Senior Crafter was
telling, and when she was finished he dangled around outside with her for a while. Never came in to hear my tales,
he didn't so much as wait long enough to share the news
about Talmar with me, left it for the Senior Crafter to relay.
All right. I went back to my own tent, tied up the charm
across my door, laid my orangestone pendant down on my
pillow to sweeten my dreams, and went to sleep. When I
woke up today, my pendant was gone and that silly citron
was lying on my travelling chest instead." In this last sentence the adventurer's voice rose and quickened. He drew a
deep breath and went on, lower and slower, "I took the
thing to my old friend the toycrafter, put it right in his
palm. He denied the whole thing, wouldn't change it back.
I warned him I'd go to the judges. He still denied it. Well,
Cousin Judge, so here I am."

"Was your charm tied across your door this morning?"

Valdart nodded. "Aye. And it's one of High Wizard
Talmar's charms, too."

"You did not actually see Torin work the transformation,
neither in your waking nor dreaming?"

"No. But who else? Who else anywhere near East'dek?"

"You sleep soundly for an adventurer," Alrathe remarked.

"Aye, when I think I'm safe among friends. When I'm
abroad where dangers have a right to spring on you, I nap
like the birds."

"And you found sleep last night with no difficulty?"

"Adventurers learn to sleep when they can." Valdart
drained his cup. "Cousin, I don't come to you judges out
of habit. Do you always question complainers as if they
were the thieves and culprits?"

"Our ideal is to question everyone equally and deliver no judgment until we've digested all their answers." The ideal was not easy, and not all judges attempted to follow it through every puzzle, but Alrathe tried to be conscientious. "I'll keep your citron for now," the judge added, pocketing it.

Torin looked at Judge Alrathe's tent again when he came out of his brother's. He could not tell at this distance whether Alrathe and Valdart were still inside or not. They might be on their way to the toymaker's booth. To keep his mind from chewing the picture of them waiting there for his return, he tried to work a pattern of what he would do if he had to wait.

He walked in preoccupation, but as he passed Merprinel's booth Laderan asked, "Well? How is Brother Talmar?"

Torin paused. "Alive, but no healthier. Except that he's sleeping. Sharys is with him."

"Ah," said Merprinel. "If Thyrna didn't gather him last night, there's a good chance he'll live through the day, and the light will help strengthen him again."

Laderan glanced at the sky. "It'll be raining any moment." His tone hinted that Merprinel was no more healer than skyreader.

Merprinel shrugged. "I have a cracked mirror, Torian," she said gently. "Mend the frame in exchange for the shards? There's no hurry, but I can give it to you now if you prefer."

He had done such work for her before. Large frames were the business of furniture crafters, but mending or carving small ones fell within toymakers' right, and the broken bits of Merprinel's fine mirrors embellished some of his most expensive gameboards. By offering him the task now, she did what she could to lend him distraction during the wait. He took it at once—she had bagged it already—but gave no promise when he would have it finished.

* * *

Laderan was still examining the mirrorcrafter's wares
when Alrathe passed by later, citron in pocket.

At discretion, judges could interview whomever they
wished as often and privately as they wished, within reason, before bringing complainant and accused together for
judgment. Wishing to speak with Torin alone, Alrathe had
given Valdart the customary cautions and sent him about
his pastime. The judge felt under no particular pressure of
haste: although in kindness the toymaker should not be
kept waiting too long, in kindness also he might relish a
few extra moments. Sometimes the most charitable course
was hard to feel out.

Merprinel wore the slightly bored and yet harried look
of a crafter waiting for a difficult buyer to decide on a
small purchase. So Alrathe paused for a short chat.

"The high wizard's breath seems a little easier this
morning," the judge said after simple hellos. Seeing Talmar's curtain supple, Alrathe had stepped in long enough
to exchange a few murmurs with his nurse.

"So Torin told us a while ago," said Merprinel.

"No," Laderan corrected her. "He said his brother was
no better, only sleeping."

"Sleep's a good sign in itself," said the judge. "Now
he's lasted the first night, we may hope he recovers, however slowly."

Laderan grunted. "Clear sunlight would help, and we're
not likely to see it today."

But Merprinel smiled at the judge as if in thanks for
seconding her own opinion. "I hope," she remarked, glancing at Laderan again, "the rain doesn't begin in fast splatters. I'd like to get my showledge inside with the mirrors
dry."

Laderan seemed to understand the hint, but begrudg-
ingly. "I've narrowed the choice to three," he said, point-
ing.

They were a pinkish tinted mirror in rosewood frame, a
purplish one in lightwood frame stained deeper purple, and

an orange-brown tinted one in goldenwood frame. All three mirrors were small, all three frames wide. "You don't want these for skyreading work?" Alrathe inquired with a surprise there seemed little use in hiding.

"A gift for my apprentice," said Laderan. "She'll turn full skyreader soon enough."

"Iris has always seemed interested in study," the judge suggested. "She might prefer an untinted one, with more mirror than wood." Also, Merprinel had to buy the frames, so that larger mirrors in small frames gave her more profitable sales.

"Iris can go on using my tools as long as she stays in my tower," said Laderan. "I've been trying to convince her that's her best plan. Better than looking for a tower of her own somewhere else and probably ending up sharing one with some other senior skyreader whose ways she'd have to get used to all over again."

"Not a marriage token, Father Laderan?" said Merprinel. He gave her a sharp glance, but she went on mischievously. "Here's the best piece I have for the marriage bed." She opened a drawer in the base of her showledge, and produced a double mirror. Both panes were square and joined where two points touched; the jointure was deep and so cut as to form an optical illusion as to which point penetrated the other. The mirrors had a pale golden cast and the frame was blackwood decorated with gold leaf and set with chips of ivory.

"Unh," said the skyreader. "I might as well try to buy that orangestone pendant whoever brought back from beyond the ocean."

"Valdart?" asked the judge.

"Aye. The young toymaker's friend."

Alrathe slipped hand in pocket to pinch the citron. "You've seen this orangestone pendant, Cousin?"

"Yesterday evening. Merchant Kara was trying to buy it from him. A teasing rascal, that sprout." Laderan shook his head and glanced at Merprinel as if insinuating she was another. "He let the merchant hold it, handle it, offer for it, but wouldn't sell. Sun was on the horizon by then, made the thing look that much prettier."

Alrathe nodded. To press for further details here would verge on an ill-mannered public discussion of comparative prices and crafting, or on the appearance of gossip; when judges indulged in gossip, rumors could grow into undesirable suspicions. But private meetings with Laderan, Merprinel, and Kara might prove useful. How much of the business between adventurer and merchant had Laderan seen while strolling around the fairground yesterday after leaving the Scholars' Pavilion? How widely had Valdart shown the pendant? How valuable was the thing in itself? Among Alrathe's most troublesome handicaps was a hasty concept of how rarity balanced craftwork in establishing just prices from area to area.

Living simply, preferring transient to stealable luxuries, the judge made an exception today and used the money-gems that had been set aside for last night's storytelling to purchase a small mirror, quickly selected, simply framed but of exquisite clarity. Then Alrathe bade them good day and went on, stirring a number of thoughts round and round one another.

It was hard to believe the possibility of Torin's guilt. Still, no person could ever fully understand another, not even those who practised sharing their thoughts. Understanding one's self was difficult enough; few managed it fully before the time to put on their harvest colors.

In an effort to make up for other deficiencies in knowledge and understanding, Alrathe had studied the oldest writings in the libraries of Horodek, Bavardek, Mirodek and Karian, Lyn Forest and Trelder Between-towns. The oldest writings were copies of copies, much translated, often unidentifiable as history, poetry, or extravagant and sometimes ugly tall tales. The race seemed to have traveled some distance along the gradual climb toward tranquility since those times when the original records were written, but the business of choosing life mates could still twist people down unexpected sidetrails. Could Laderan, who would be wearing harvest colors in ten years, really hope to marry his young apprentice? This season with its cooling weather and prospect of winter nights seemed to inspire marriage-bed plans.

Like most individuals similarly circumstanced, Alrathe had decided early against trying for life mate and children. Never tempted to change that decision, the judge felt even less acquainted with emotions among chooser and would-be chosen than with the values of luxuries. And yet, mused Alrathe, I dare judge in these matters between persons who know what it is to climb over and around such boulders.

But they came and paid for judgments, and perhaps the race climbed higher and faster by gazing at ideals of pure justice, hard as ideals might be to apply when the culprit seemed in other traits more gentle than the complainer or when the motivations were clear as Merprinel's mirrors to understand. Happily, while always compelled by conscience to give judgment as they determined the abstract right, judges remained free to fit corrective measures to the circumstances of each case. Alrathe would not have cared to be a magic-monger called to judge a fellow student in that discipline, with its code of fixed penalties.

In the present case, the judge knew both Torin and Sharys far more closely than the complainant Valdart. That in itself demanded wariness against giving the adventurer's charge insufficient consideration.

But was the citron really the pendant transformed? Valdart had only the argument that he had gone to sleep with the one on his pillow and wakened with the other on his traveling chest. A magic-monger effecting a transformation would have run less risk of awakening Valdart by leaving the object where it lay near his head. A lay person making a simple exchange would have risked less, after successfully removing pendant from pillow, by leaving the citron elsewhere.

A citron for an orangestone pendant? In some places, Alrathe guessed, it might be a fair trade. In some places, indeed, the citron might be more expensive: in the neighborhood where the pendants were made, for instance, if it lay too far north for growing citrons. Here, however, while citrons were among the most expensive fruit, Alrathe assumed a piece of bluemetal and orangestone jewelry would be priced much higher. Citrons were available at most fairs hereabouts; orangestones set in crafted bluemetal were seen perhaps once every three to five years. The trade appeared negligible, almost insulting.

Moreover, Valdart's tent had been protected by one of High Wizard Talmar's charms. Only a magic-monger—or Torin—could have untied it with harmful intent. Alrathe knew of no one else near East'dek who had the necessary magical skill. Torin was exceptional. Within living memory, only two others between Mirodek and Varodek had started and then failed to continue along the trail of magic, and both were incompetent conjurers finally rejected as unsuitable. One had died a few years ago of old age, the other had turned adventurer and not been seen for several seasons. Of the three studies, magic was the one most reluctant to lose its adherents.

By Valdart's statement, Torin had already refused or failed to untransform the citron. If one of Vathilda's family had done it, all three women might share the secret and refuse to change the fruit back. Talmar's illness eliminated him from being asked to make the test, as surely as it appeared to eliminate him from suspicion. There was a chance that Torin, if guilty, would do for a judge what he had refused to do for an adventurer, old friend or not, whom he had injured. Alrathe thought the possibility slight. The toymaker had been raised a magic-monger, and if conscience did not move him to confession, neither probably would awe for the student classes. Vathilda, Hilshar, and Sharys, still and ever students, were even less likely to bend in awe before a fellow scholar. Indeed, the judge could not be sure that the old sorceress might not in pure mischief transform a genuine citron into an orangestone pendant, if she thought the matter silly enough. Sharys, whom both men wished for a chosen, might have younger and deeper reasons for a similar prank; and Sharys had seen the real pendant, so that Valdart might not succeed in recognizing her mischievous transformation as counterfeit. Vathilda and Hilshar might have seen the original also.

The only sure quick test appeared to be eating the citron. Alrathe smiled wryly. If this fruit were in fact transformed orangestone and bluemetal, the sure test would result in its permanent loss and in grief to the tester's organs. Allowing the puzzle to remain unsolved would be preferable.

That aspect made the affair all the more unsettling. A magic-monger bent only on depriving Valdart of a valuable marriage token, or on playing him a joke, should have transformed the pendant into something equally inedible. Alrathe did not want to suspect that these emotions of desire for a chosen mate could twist the toymaker into causing an old friend bodily pain, maybe illness as grave as Talmar's.

If the citron were a transformation, it should eventually change back of itself. Or, if it were Vathilda's work, it could be a spell too tight for the toymaker even to sense. Or Valdart might have hidden the pendant and crafted a lie to discredit Torin in this effort for Sharys. That was an easier suspicion than Torin's guilt, but no less ugly.

Alrathe sighed and pinched the citron again, wishing, as always when beginning with a puzzle or ending with a judgment, for deeper and clearer knowledge of all things.

Five

FINDING THE JUDGE already at his tent might have relieved Torin's tension. Since Alrathe was not there yet, he had to use the wait to best advantage, and since Alrathe might come at any moment, he had to work fast.

Uncomfortably aware that the best immediate task might be his daily grooming, he stored Merprinel's cracked mirror safely away and retrieved Talmar's globe from beneath the blanket. It had continued its review all the time it lay there, and still showed much the same scene: High Wizard Talmar alone in his tent, gesturing over the curved surface, causing the sequence to skip and stutter. The imaged light seemed less insistent, as if the day were nearer twilight. Dawn twilight, it must be, and the scene was almost certainly Talmar making a last rehearsal yesterday morning before the scholars' banquet.

The globe did not record present events while showing past. They had proved this yesterday afternoon, when Judge Alrathe watched three successive reviews of the banquet, calling Torin every few hours from beside Talmar's bed and asking him to repeat the gestures. Vathilda refused to learn them, and Hilshar followed the hint. Sharys might have been willing to learn, but she was only a conjurer and if the grandmother judged scorn of Talmar's new technique the best treatment for his boasting sickness, the granddaughter must obey. Alrathe relinquished the globe only when they took Talmar at last to his own tent, a few hours before midnight, and left him waiting for the Harvest Spirit.

Between his sense of need for haste, his doubt whether he should not groom first, and the confusion of Talmar's rehearsal, which seemed to include many experimental variations, Torin needed three attempts before he could repeat the sequence learned yesterday.

After the third attempt, as he lifted his hand away from the globe, it reflected a pair of hands holding it, faint light limning the spaces between spread fingers. They did not seem to be Torin's hands. He was deciding they were Talmar's, when a patch of fog appeared on one side of the globe. It seemed to remain steady inside a turning, like a bit of something floating on the surface of a cup of tea that remains in approximately the same position to a person turning the cup on the table, as if only the cup moves and not its contents. The area not fogged reflected a jumble of intermixed shapes and colors, impossible to distinguish or identify. Torin feared he had made the gestures wrong.

The confusion lasted perhaps sixty or seventy breaths, which Torin tried to inhale and exhale smoothly. Then the globe flashed white. He blinked. Talmar must have illuminated it, but only for a moment. After the brief brightness from within, the muddled images returned, whirling around the befogged patch.

Then at last the fog faded, the reflection steadied except for a rough up-down movement, and Torin made out that the scene was Talmar lying prone in his tent, holding the globe near his chest.

So the jumble had been some result of Talmar's sickness?

Torin seemed to have watched a long and a short time at
once, and the judge would be coming. The toymaker rose
with a sense of belated haste, went and relieved himself,
returned and gestured over the globe again, this time starting its review easily. Feeling a little hunger, he shelled the
cracked boiled egg and ate it in three bites to be rid of it
and its egg odor. He closed the traveling chest, arranged
the globe on it in a nest of wadded towel, set up basin,
pitcher, soap, and unguent, creamed off his day-old beard,
and washed, glancing continually at the globe. It showed
the same confusion as the first time. He moved so quickly
that he finished grooming before the flash. He put on clean
tunic, wiped the globe of splashes it had sustained from his
washbasin, changed trousers and tied his belt. The review
reached the steadying moment.

He carried his brazier outside, kindled it, dropped the
eggshell into the flames. He returned inside, lit a cake of
incense to soak up the lingering smell of boiled egg, gestured the globe back once more to the start of what it had to
show. After watching a few moments and seeing nothing
different, he went outside again to check the brazier.

Raindrops started falling. The coals were not burned
down enough to take the brazier inside, but, like most good
brazier sets, Torin's followed the pattern designed a few
generations ago by Kaderian, one of the very few crafters
ever to wear a four-syllable name. Torin lifted the coal pan
by its insulated handles, set it on the ground, and turned
the stand upside down over it to shelter it from rain while
allowing the smoky vapors to escape.

As he stood, he saw the judge.

Like most people, Alrathe must be wearing a charm-
disk to turn raindrops away within a few inches of the
body. Rain stopped little of a fair's back-and-forth traffic,
but it drove business inside tents or, as with most of the
animal trade, beneath wide awnings. In turning drops away
from a body and and its immediate clothing, the charm
created a surrounding sheath of thicker spray to wet anything unprotected towards which the person reached out.

"Cousin Toymaker!" Alrathe's greeting sounded friendly.

"Cousin Judge." Torin held up the doorcurtain while Alrathe ducked inside.

Torin followed nervously. His life had included few experiences with judgments and none with Alrathe's work style, but a judge's interview could resemble a word-whipping, and judges occasionally told persons they suspected of lying, evading questions, or improperly searching their memories, to hold their arms out unsupported like naughty children. He half considered leaving his doorcords untied as if by oversight, for without the signal that those within did not wish to be disturbed, someone might interrupt the session. Dilys, perhaps, or Ulrad and Kara, who still owed for the toys they had taken yesterday. If he had truly forgotten . . . but courtesy required him to tie the cords, so he did.

As he dropped the curtain, light flashed behind him. He turned and saw Alrathe looking at the globe beside the washbasin.

"Yes," said Torin, "It's my brother's. I don't know how it reached my tent—I found it when I woke this morning."

"Strange," said Alrathe. "I visited Talmar's tent on my way. He's sleeping, which may be a good sign."

"I know. I went there this morning, too." Torin wondered if the fact that he had broken his wait would impress the judge against him. "I guessed I'd have time before you came." Worse! Depending on what Valdart had told Alrathe, the judge might not have known the toymaker was forewarned. Well, the judge knew now, so Torin went on, "But that citron *is* a citron, Cousin Judge. I have no idea what happened to Valdart's pendant."

Alrathe pulled out a citron and tossed it to the toymaker. Taken by surprise, Torin failed to catch it, recovered it from the floor rugs.

The judge sighed. "It's the same citron. Would you be willing to eat it?"

Feeling a blush, Torin lifted the fruit to his mouth.

"Enough!" said the judge. "Toss it back. I'm not sure I could comfortably afford to repay Valdart even for a citron."

Torin tossed it back with relief.

Alrathe caught it easily, pocketed it, and picked up Talmar's globe. "For the moment, this interests me more. Sharys said nothing to me about its disappearance."

"I'm not sure it'd be very important in her thoughts, unless Talmar woke and asked for it. His health seems to be her great concern right now."

"A true healer, with true healers' concentration," said Alrathe before Torin had time to brood on what her new concern might mean in terms of her eventual marriage choice. "The image seems to have settled," Alrathe went on.

"Yes. This is the second, no, third time I've made it review. It's always the same. The misted patch, confused images, flash of light, more confusion, then it settles and shows my brother waiting for the Harvest Spirit."

"Most poets agree that the past does not change."

Torin blushed again. "I may have made the gestures wrong. Some mistake of mine could have muddled the images. By accident."

"Well, you're more nearly magic-monger than I." Alrathe brought the globe to Torin. "May I ask you to gesture again?"

Torin obliged. Carrying the globe, Alrathe sat on the bed. Torin hesitated a moment, then cleared the top of the travelling chest and used it for a chair.

"Had the fault been with your gestures," said Alrathe, "would the image settle at last?"

"It might be some result of his sickness. Breathing his delirium into the reflection."

Alrathe turned the globe. "What dreams might it give a dying person, the fear of achievement lost through lack of anyone to continue the work?"

"But not me!" Torin slumped, elbows on knees. "Surely another magic-monger."

"I doubt Vathilda would want the task. Now that she's scoffed at its value, she might feel that investigating Talmar's technique would break faith with her own. Her daughter's a self-professed workaday magician more in rhythm with the practical than the theoretical. And Sharys is still only a conjurer at nineteen."

"There must be others. The study's overcrowded. I'm willing to show the gestures to any magic-monger. Without charge. The Supreme Mage herself might be interested."

"But Talmar seems to want you. Perhaps he believes his brother's mind must work most like his own."

"Or it's only family pride—family selfishness!" cried Torin. Then he remembered that his brother might be near death, and hung his head. "Forgive my anger."

"I'm not trying to transform you, Cousin Toymaker. Only to find the possible current of your brother's thoughts. This globe hardly rolled into your tent of its own motive power."

"Sharys thought he might have softened his door last night, wanting a nurse, and someone took advantage of it to steal . . ." But a thief would have kept the globe. "Unlikely, isn't it?"

"Very." Alrathe stared into the glassy ball. "A second person may be in the tent with the high wizard. Difficult to be sure. It may be mind dictating to eyes, saying that someone else must have been with him last night. But the someone was more probably a chosen messenger than a thief. Is it possible that Talmar summoned you yourself to him with a mind-message, and you obeyed it more than half asleep?"

Torin shook his head helplessly. "I don't remember any dreams of being otherwhere than here in my own tent."

"Well, sleep business is strange and may grow even stranger in memory, though that's hard to demonstrate," mused the judge. "You dream your dreams, I mine, and neither of us has any personal recollection of the other's. No one can contradict another person's dreams. But wak-

ing events shared by more than one witness . . . There each
individual's recollection usually differs in small details or
large from everyone else's." Then, with a head shake as if
emerging from general reverie to the particular case, "But
an impressive number of poets agree in their opinion that
folk rarely do things asleep they would refuse to do
awake."

Torin did not feel comforted. If he had gone half asleep
to his brother's tent, his own will, even his own desire,
might be more wavery than he himself suspected. Also, it
raised the idea that he might have sleepwalked unremem-
bering to Valdart's tent. He wondered if he ought to mention his conversation with the animated statue, which
might contain some garbled dream memory of motive for
either or both midnight sleepwalkings.

The judge went on, "Was your own charm corded across
your door last night and this morning?"

"I tied it last night. This morning . . . I'm not sure. Valdart came in before I had gone near the doorcurtain."

"Rude, if the cords were tied. Apparently impossible for
a lay person, if the charm was knotted in."

"No. I thought of that, but the charm was only spellcast
against thievery and mischief, not rudeness. And Valdart
thought he had cause to be angry."

"Ah!" said Alrathe. "If you should decide to turn
magic-monger again perhaps you'll work on a more all-in-
clusive charm."

"It's limited because otherwise friends might not be able
to get in to help in case of accident."

Alrathe nodded. "I'll have to ask Valdart. We'll hope he
remembers so minor a detail as the charm in your doorcords."

Raindrops pattered on the cloth roof. The protective
magic against thievery and mischief did not perceive falling droplets as a menace, and few people used drycharms
against rain on their tents. Usually the sound was not uncomfortable.

"If I was last night's culprit," said Torin, "undoing charms to work mischief, I doubt the study would want me back."

Alrathe shrugged. "We have two puzzles here, Talmar's globe and Valdart's pendant, and no surety that they are connected, nor that one culprit is responsible for both. If we can even theorize a culprit, and not a messenger, in the case of the globe. . . . Well, let's hope you were not the one responsible, or we may have a true ache of a brain-tangle, the magickers and I. Would you rather be judged by judges or magickers, Cousin?"

"By judges, I think. As a common crafter."

"But not as a pure layperson. If magic does enter into this . . . Yet how could they judge you without first receiving you back as a fellow student, and could they accept you if you were guilty?" Alrathe shrugged again. "Cousin, you are unique. I remember no cases similar to yours, at least none recent enough to help guide us. But I'm far from sure that magic is involved."

"If the charms didn't work because no mischief was intended, only rudeness . . ." said Torin, trying to follow the judge's thought.

"But mischief was perceived by the complainer, if not by the charm. Then the charm's magic would appear more sensitive to intruder than to rightful owner."

"It may be more sensitive to whoever is closest." While saying this, Torin worried that he was reasoning more like magic-monger than toycrafter.

"Yes," said Alrathe, "it seems to me, lay though I am in magic, that improving our protective charms would give magickers a more practical project than making globes show—"

Talmar's globe flashed its light.

"Three puzzles," said Alrathe, "if your brother's malady counts as one. I confess I was never quite satisfied with Vathilda's identification, but until now. . ." The judge tapped Talmar's globe. "Cousin, you have your own magic globe, I believe?"

Torin sat upright and looked around. His globe was not on its stand. He thought he remembered getting it out last night, fingering it, but then he had decided to light a candle instead. He must have put the globe away. Though not as fragile as they looked, the glass balls could be broken. Magic-mongers guarded against it with a durability spell renewed daily as part of their morning meditation. The toymaker guarded against it by storing his globe in a cushion-lined box. Bending, he found the box (one of his own prenticework carvings) beside the chest, brought it up into his lap, opened it and lifted out the globe.

"Enclosed in cushions and wood all night." He shook his head. "No, mine couldn't have witnessed anything. Even if Talmar's new technique doesn't require any kind of preliminary spellcasting to make the globes remember."

"Bothersome. Had yours been positioned to see, we might have had the answer to one puzzle, at least, in a few hours. But if you could find a way to pass back through years in a short time . . . You mentioned yesterday that your brother suffered a similar fit at his First Name-Lengthening feast. I assume your globe might have helped light that occasion."

"Probably. But he showed me nothing of skipping back to some chosen moment."

"And we can't wait twenty years for the scene. So unless you can refine your brother's technique this afternoon, we must depend on your memory."

"My memory?" said Torin. "It's not a pleasant memory for me, Cousin Judge. I've let it molder unstudied."

"One might also say, relatively unembellished by later mindcasts. All I want from your memory is what foods you and your family ate and, if possible, what foods you transformed them out of."

Hope cut sharply into the toymaker's lungs. "You suspect food sensitivity?"

"I have all along. It was not my right to question Mother Vathilda's ideas, not until I could find some reason to make the high wizard's sickness an affair for judgework. This puzzle of Talmar's globe may give me that right."

"Food sensitivity. That should pass of itself!"

"So should the boasting sickness, I think, now the worst
appears to be over. But we can guess what boulders a reputation for glory-choking will roll into Cousin Talmar's
climb for honor."

"We can guess." Torin slipped his globe back into its
cushions and gently closed the box. "I'll try to search my
memory, Cousin Judge."

"Write out a list, if you can." Alrathe stood. "It's all I
ask for now."

Torin also rose, setting down the box. "My brazier
should be ready to heat water soon. Or I have pear cordial."

"Thank you, not this time. I hope we'll drink together
more cheerfully when our puzzles are solved." Alrathe
handed Torin the high wizard's globe. The image had settled to Talmar alone on his bed. "Let it continue showing
its review. As I understand the technique, that will save
whatever it saw last night for whenever I may want to look
at the scene again. Or it may reach yesterday afternoon
while one more study of the feast might still be useful."

Torin nodded. Cradling the globe in one arm, he drew
back the doorcurtain and untied the cords.

At the doorway, the judge paused and put a hand on the
toymaker's shoulders. Torin was rather short, and stooping
a little just now as he held the curtain. The judge was
slightly taller.

"Cousin," said Alrathe, "I also suggest that you reexam-
ine whatever dreams you may have experienced last
night."

Torin nodded again. "Cousin Judge, I'll try."

He watched Alrathe move away, crimson robe unspat-
tered, between other charm-protected fairgoers and wetten-
ing tents. Standard magical theory postulated that the
wearer's own bodily heat helped activate personal drycharms. Torin looked at his brazier, decided it was not yet
ready to bring inside, dropped the doorcurtain and returned

to sit on his bed. He was not quite sure whether Alrathe had taken him into confidence as an assistant, or already reached some judgment on him. Sighing, he lifted Talmar's globe. When displaying the past it showed no hint of superimposed present reflection. He laid it carefully on his pillow, got his own smaller globe out of the box once more, sat and looked at it for a few moments, then made Talmar's gestures over it.

He lifted his hand away and watched its reflection go back through the series in reverse. So the technique did not require preliminary treatment of the globe.

If Talmar's delirium had caused the period of confused images, a globe might respond to the thoughts of whoever was practising this technique upon it. In that case, there might be some mental way to guide it back and pick out an hour it had witnessed years ago.

Torin shivered. His mind seemed to be working at this with the interest of a magicker. He felt caught in paradox. But he repeated the gestures over his globe and held it in the path of his exhaled breath as he tried thinking back to his brother's First Name-Lengthening.

$\mathfrak{S}$ix

MENTALLY REENUMERATING WHOM to interview, and deciding that soonest would be best with Vathilda and her family, Alrathe walked briskly back to the scholars' area, observing on the way that Merprinel, like other booth-keepers, already had her business snug inside.

Approaching Sharys in the sick wizard's tent on an errand of judgecraft seemed rude, even though the curtain was still pliable. But judges had the right to employ surprise as a tool.

Talmar was still laboriously sleeping. Sharys bent over him, her cloth-padded fingers hovering near his face. She did not seem to notice that someone else had just come into the tent.

"Cousin Sharys," said the judge.

At that she started, looked around and up. "Cousin Alrathe?"

"I hope to leave you again quickly." The judge stepped closer, held out the citron, and nodded at the wizard. "These, I believe, are among his favorite delicacies?"

The conjurer took it. "Yes. I made that whole platter of them yesterday. He must have eaten ten or twelve." She blinked twice, and a tear rolled down her left cheek. "Is this a real one?"

"There's some doubt."

She frowned.

"I had thought," the judge went on, "that you might sense it."

She curled her fingers around the citron and closed her eyes, but opened them almost at once. "Cousin Alrathe, have you come here as a friend or a judge or a . . . a . . . It's not any time for jokes."

"Would you risk feeding that fruit to the high wizard?"

"No. I wouldn't risk feeding him anything but broth and sops and cordials and water. But I'd risk eating it myself."

Alrathe sighed. "I've come as judge. A complainer brought that to me this morning with the claim it was transformed orangestone."

Her eyes widened as if in horror, then closed again and she sat in concentration for several minutes, her hand tight around the citron. She shook her head.

"You'd still risk eating it yourself?"

"No. I *think* it's real fruit, but I'm only a conjurer. Grandmother was already a sorceress by this age."

"And then she suffered her own case of Choking Glory?"

"When she was . . . twenty-three, I think. A few years after my mother was born. What can that have to do with this?"

"More things connect with one another than we sometimes guess." Alrathe conceived judges' work as searching out the interrelationships, never as trying to isolate one piece of mischief from its total setting. "Have you guessed who my complainant is?"

She thought for a moment and shrugged. "Valdart, I suppose." Her tone surprised Alrathe—less than casual, almost annoyed.

"Valdart had planned to give you that piece of jewelry

as a marriage token. He seemed confident you would accept it."

"Oh, I'm tired of them both!" She brushed back some strands of golden hair that had strayed across her forehead. "Making a—what would you call it?—some sort of gameboard out of it. Why can't they leave me untroubled to make my own choice? So they've told you all about it, too."

"As judge, not as gossip. And as judge, I have found no reason so far to believe this particular gameboard is of Torin's design."

"I hope not. Not with his own brother so sick. But after yesterday morning . . . Talmar might not be so much to Valdartak. . . ." She paused and pinched the citron, frowning again.

"It may not be the adventurer's design, either. It may be the handiwork of some unknown trickster."

"Who? And why?" She shook her head and thrust the citron back into Alrathe's hand. "Cousin, he's trying to make you one more piece on the gameboard. Tell him I'm glad Torin—Torinel—warned me to wait." She began retying her pale green hairband. Her fingers trembled slightly.

"Yesterday's citrons," said the judge. "What did you make them out of?"

"Potatoes. I thought you saw them untransform. My transformations were the first to unknit. Not that it matters, only if I were a better magicker . . . I don't care about transformations and performances, but to be able to heal more skillfully!"

Alrathe wondered how overcautious Vathilda's Choking Glory might have made her daughter and granddaughter in their own study. "It could matter a great deal if this is simple food sensitivity."

She snatched the significance at once. "Grandmother says it's boasting sickness," she said, but hope showed in her upward glance.

"And perhaps I have no right to question her. But who

should know better how glory-choking can stop the climb to honors?"

"Grandmother says there are more important peaks to climb. I'm sure he's eaten all those delicacies before. But the base foods!" she exclaimed softly. "Of course. Transformations almost always retain some quality of the original, and my poor weak transformations . . ."

Alrathe was glad she had thought of it but disturbed that she blamed her lack of skill. "Need the fault have been clumsiness in the transformation? By his brother's memory, Talmar suffered such a fit in childhood. His own parents, high wizard and mage, would have prepared the meal then."

"The goldfruits were potatoes, too," said Sharys. "Larger potatoes. I sorted carefully so I wouldn't need to work with size. The dates and olives were carrots cut small, the powderflour wafers were cabbage leaves, the dewmelons were small whole cabbages, the whitenuts were parched corn, the jewelberries were dried peas . . . But if he were sensitive to any of the delicacies, he wouldn't have eaten them. But some combination? That no one's noticed until now because it doesn't happen very often?"

Alrathe nodded eagerly. "Cousin, if you could make a list, mark what foods he favored most. I can perhaps help there, having watched it over again yesterday in his globe —citrons, dewmelon, dates, goldcobs."

"The goldcobs were natural," said Sharys.

Talmar choked and she whirled back to him, not looking up again until she was satisfied he still slept and breathed relatively safely. "Can't you check the globe again today?"

"When it reviews its way back to the correct hour. But the images are tiny and such things as which wine is poured are not always clear. His own memory might be the most reliable of all."

She nodded. "I'll explain. When he wakes, if he's strong enough. Oh, Talmariak, if it *is* only a sensitivity!"

Alrathe felt considerable satisfaction on leaving the high wizard's tent. Talmar might both survive and be able to climb the peak of honors, after all. And, thought the judge, I believe that the problem of his globe is no very great puzzle. We may hope Talmar himself will not object to enlightening us when he recovers sufficient strength, at least as to his own method and motive. He might not wish to reveal his messenger, or why cloud and confuse the scene (assuming it was done on purpose)? But perhaps no one really need seek that particular answer.

The marriage toy puzzle, however: that was more ticklish.

Vathilda's tent faced Talmar's. Its doorcurtain hung supple. Alrathe crossed the footway and entered.

Hilshar sat alone, sorting little things that Alrathe recognized as belonging to the periphery of magic, the feats meant to please a lay audience and scorned by many more advanced or pretentious students: tiny globes, scarves, nets, phials of colored liquid.

"Cousin," said Hilshar, looking up. She was a placid woman, a shock-cushion between her sharp mother and her intense daughter. The judge wondered if Hilshar's calm had been purchased with hard climbing or if the family temper had mercifully skipped a generation.

"Cousin Magician." Alrathe put the citron down before her in the middle of a small, empty ringwood frame. "What do you think of this?"

She picked it up. "If it's one of my daughter's transformations, I'm proud of it. All the rest unknit themselves by yesterday evening."

"Are you sure it's a transformation?"

As Torin and Sharys had done, Hilshar curled her fingers round the fruit and closed her eyes. "No," she said at last, "it's real. Are you testing me, Cousin Judge, or is it a gift for poor Talmar?"

"A test, but of the citron." Alrathe sat and told her of the adventurer's complaint. Although she listened with her customary calm, she appeared to have known nothing about the transformation or trade of the pendant. She did not interrupt with so much as a wordless exclamation, but her eyes opened a little wider.

At the end of Alrathe's brief account, Hilshar sighed and shook her head. "I would not like that adventurer for a daughter's husband."

"Then it sounds to you like a trick of Valdart's to discredit his friend?"

"The citron's real, as far as my skill can test it. I'll say no more. I couldn't say as much as that to Sharys, but I hope her choice goes elsewhere."

"To the toymaker?"

"So Mother hopes. My own hopes . . . But I think my daughter is one of those who must choose her own guides or climb her trail alone."

"I wouldn't presume to advise her. But whatever the truth of this trick, who played it upon whom, Sharys should know before making her decision."

"Aye. Although how it may swing her choice . . . Cousin Judge, my own husband was a clothcrafter. Mother thought crafters would make the best mates for a family like ours, in danger of the boasting sickness. It was not a comfortable marriage. He turned adventurer, hired his work to a merchant travelling west. He left promising to visit us every second or third year. He never returned. It's a poor, tiny gage to measure them by, so I say nothing to my daughter. But, well, Torin's a steady young man, and I'd rather see her choose him than the adventurer. Still, his being half crafter and half magicker, I'm not sure if that would make their climb together easier or harder."

So Hilshar's tranquility had been purchased. Alrathe nodded. Further reassurance was unnecessary. Judges often became the recipients of spontaneous unburdenings, which could happen only when the tellers already trusted their listeners' discretion.

"Mother Vathilda is taking advantage of the rain to arrange a magic performance in the Scholars' Tent," Hilshar went on. "To earn money for buying Talmar natural comforts. If any magic-monger here can tell you for sure whether this is a real citron or a transformation, it's she."

Alrathe thanked Hilshar, took back the citron, and set out for the Scholars' Tent.

Seven

THE SOUND OF rain on her tent woke Dilys the storycrafter.

She had needed a long time to fall asleep last night, which would have made lying under her blankets dozing in the morning rain very pleasant. But the same thoughts that had kept her awake were waiting, ready to surface again even as she woke.

She got up, washed and dressed in haste. The morning still felt early, but clouds and rain could warp human time-sense. Pulling back the curtain, she looked out and nodded. Hard to guess where above the clouds the sun might be, but no one stood in front of the Storytellers' Pavilion waiting for the cords to be untied, and the number of fairgoers who walked from tent to tent was too small for midmorning bustle but too large for midday when folk would shelter to eat their meal.

Dilys had scheduled herself for the day's first storytelling. The early afternoon hour was not enviable. The audience wandered in whenever they finished eating. The entry price remained a single large stone throughout this one session—in fair weather some stragglers even objected to paying that, preferring to wait and come in when the next teller began. Wise storycrafters filled such first sessions with short snippet-tales, saving long ones for later. This made good sense, but Dilys found it tedious work. Nevertheless, when as senior crafter she naturally received the best evening hour, balancing it with the worst afternoon hour was only fair. Also, it made sense to draw as many listeners as possible as soon as possible to the Storytellers' Pavilion. Any senior who refused the first session almost invariably took the second for that reason.

The rain should help make this a profitable afternoon, but meanwhile Dilys had other concerns. Postponing breakfast, she merely swallowed a few mouthfuls of cold water and wine. To guard against throat phlegm she slipped her protective disk around her neck, but did not take her drycharm. The rain seemed warm for late autumn, and her cloak was still new enough that the wool resisted drops for a while. Dilys liked to recreate, when possible and not too inconvenient, what folk must have experienced in the days before life was protected with so many charms. It helped her storycrafting. Besides, this fairground was not large. She should be at the toymaker's tent before the rain had much chance to soak through. She pinned her cloak with the carved brookstone brooch she had bought from Torin several years ago, pulled up her hood, stepped out into the rain, tied her doorcords around the tentcharm in the special knot that signalled fellow storycrafters she would be available in a few hours, and set off.

Torin's doorcords hung untied, so Dilys went right in. She found him standing with his back to the door, holding out his arms unsupported at his sides.

She started to back out again, but she must have let in a draft, and one of her unfastened cloak toggles clicked on his dangling tentcharm. He shivered, dropped his arms, and turned.

She tried a smile. "You haven't been naughty again?"

"I hope not."

She saw he was blushing and regretted her attempt to banter. It was the kind of teasing she herself would not have liked. "I'm sorry. It's not because of . . . How is your brother?"

"Alive. He was sleeping this morning. Not too easily, but it's something. No drycharm?"

She took off her cloak and shook it carefully so as to limit splattering to a small area near the door. "I've been told that when the people in my tales about old times walk through rain, my listeners can almost feel it on their own bodies."

"Well, your stories are popular anyway." He grinned.

"Like your toys."

He sighed.

"Torinel, do you want to go back to magic?"

"I don't know." He turned to his brazier, where a small kettle was heating. "The water's near the boil. What will you drink?"

"Roseblend." She spread her cloak over part of the floormat, somewhat away from the entrance, and sat cross-legged near the bed, fingering her brookstone brooch. "If your brother gets well, there'll be no need at all for you to go back—not that there was anyway. Not unless you want to."

"If this is boasting sickness, his climb stops here. Mine, maybe, would not."

"You don't think a man like Talmar would appreciate seeing his brother climb on past him to higher glories?"

"He might. If it meant the general honor of the family."

"He's not too young to marry," said the storyteller.

"No. But once a strain of glory-choking appears . . . Look at Mother Vathilda and her line."

Dilys flicked the brooch down into her lap, interlinked her fingers, and squeezed them tight. "But your line would be untainted?" she said. Even if you married Vathilda's granddaughter? she thought. Aloud, she added, "And your children might want to pick the study up again—especially if their mother's a magicker. So you could very well let it skip one generation with a comfortable conscience and keep on making toys. What kind of sense is the conjurer showing in her choice today?"

"I don't believe she's thinking very much about either of us. It's Talmar who concerns her right now." He confided it without hesitation or embarrassment toward his visitor. In a way, she was proud he felt free to speak with her of such things.

He poured the boiling water and mixed in the herbs, two cups of roseblend. They both enjoyed its sweet-sour bite; their taste preferences were very similar. He brought her one cup, then sat on the bed, put his cup down in front of him, and stared at it. "But would my line be untainted? I've been proud, Dilysin. Very proud of my craftwork, very proud of turning aside to follow my own trail."

"Proud enough to choke on it?"

He shook his head.

"And your parents? Did they ever glory-choke?"

"No. But maybe our mother feared it in herself. Maybe that's part of the reason she turned wanderer when she might have been named Elder Mage."

"Did she ever say that was why she left?"

Again he shook his head. "She might have feared to worry us."

The storyteller tapped her fingers impatiently on her cup. "Or she might not even have been tempted by the Elder Mageship. Mage-Mother Talysidore might be wandering because she really prefers it—because she doesn't have any of that kind of pride, not because she has too much. I don't think she'd keep silent if she thought it was a danger in the line, I think she'd have warned her children specifically. As for being proud of your toys, why shouldn't you be? They're worth it. And as for putting your mark on each of them, every good crafter who wants to earn an independent livelihood had better do that. It's no more than my bright tunics and picture-belts to make people remember me and come back to buy my stories again."

Torin looked around at the showledge of toys on the

floor beside his traveling chest. "They say almost everyone wants to change occupations sometime in life."

"Well." She sipped the hot roseblend. "And most of those who try it seem to muddle it and go back to their old callings in a few years. But you may be lucky. I imagine you could change back and be as good as a magicker as you are a toycrafter. If that's what you want."

"I don't know. I don't think it is. But I'm not sure. I haven't tired of toycrafting yet, not for longer than a day or two at a time. But I've tried some experiments that were, well, unwise. Like the toy lyre."

"That music-crafter never needed to call in a judge on you," said Dilys.

"But he did have sound arguments. Toy musical instruments could have spoiled children's ears for real music and cut into the true music-craft. I should have thought of that myself."

"Exactly. All he needed was to come to you and point it out, and you'd have stopped."

"Especially as the experiment wasn't finding any buyers." Torin smiled wryly. "But maybe these experiments are an indication. Maybe I'm more restless than I know. If someday I run out of rightful new things to try, variations in technique . . ."

"I grow restless at least once or twice a year," she told him. "At one time or another, I've tried peeking into everyone's workshop. I've spent whole days and nights playing at gardencraft, skyreading, weaving—I unravelled that effort and used the thread for mending. You've seen that lopsided pot from my claycrafting efforts, and maybe sometime I'll show you a pair of very strange-looking shoes that were a true waste of old leather. But whenever I try to go longer than three days without making or telling a story, I start losing touch with my lungs."

"I think I may have two sets of lungs. Or my lungs are breathing out of rhythm with each other."

"Well," said Dilys. "I've sometimes thought of pestering you to teach me toycrafting. Turn magic-monger, Torinel, but take me for a toymaking prentice, and we'll both have two callings."

"There isn't enough time in a season." But he looked back at her with a more cheerful grin.

"There's enough time in a lifetime."

"Everything you dabble at connects with your story-crafting, Dilysin. Like walking through rain without a dry-charm. But magic and toycrafting . . . There's no proper relationship."

She drank more herbwater.

"Dilysin," he said, "what rumors have you heard today?"

"None. I just bundled out of my tent into yours."

He sighed. "You might be able to carve this into a story. The marriage toy Valdart meant to give Sharilys, that blue-metal and orangestone pendant, disappeared from his tent last night and an unwanted citron appeared instead."

"Valdart's famous pendant from beyond the western ocean? The one he's been using to tease selected merchants and dazzle selected children?"

"Yes. He thinks I slipped in and transformed it. Maybe I did, sleepwalking. He's called in the judge."

Her fingers tightened around the cup, but loosened again because it was still hot. "Is that why you were standing arms-out just now?"

"Not exactly. Well, in a way. They say it helps focus your thoughts. That's why judges use the technique some-times, isn't it? To hear reliable answers?"

"Cousin Alrathe told you to hold out your arms and then didn't stay to direct the process?"

"No. Alrathe seemed to treat me more like a helper." He set down his cup and twisted around on his bed, reaching backwards. When he moved, Dilys could see two magic globes propped against his pillow. He touched the smaller globe, then shook his head and picked up the larger. Squinting, Dilys made out that they seemed to be reflecting different scenes.

Torin handed her the globe. She turned it, staring at the

barely visible interior of a tent that did not appear to be the one they sat in.

"Talmar's globe," Torin explained. "He took it last night for a deathbed toy. That must be what it's showing now. He finally found his technique for making globes show past reflections."

She nodded. Torin had sometimes told her about his brother's efforts, and she had heard rumors yesterday. "So that's the new trick that stirred up his Choking Glory."

"If it is Choking Glory."

Dilys looked up at her friend. "Ah? I thought that was the whole problem."

"Alrathe thinks it might be food sensitivity. In a few hours, Talmar's globe should work its way back to yesterday's banquet. It doesn't seem to watch or record present reflections while showing old ones." Torin waved his arm at Talmar's globe—a conversational gesture, not a magical one. "Meanwhile, I've been experimenting with my own globe." He reached round again and rolled it to him, lifting it to his knees. "If I could find some way to pick out reflections at will, stir up very old scenes, twenty years old . . ." He shook his head. "If I could do that so easily, it'd make a clear sign I should go back to magic."

Dilys looked at Torin's small globe, which showed a pretty swirl of colors. "Your experiments came to nothing."

"Nothing useful."

She did not point out how short a time he must have been at it. Crafting instinct, not frustration, might have stopped his morning's work in magic. "So you were holding out your arms to concentrate your own memory of whatever happened twenty years ago. Sometimes telling things aloud is the best thought-focusing toy."

He turned the globe without seeming to watch it. "You said you haven't heard any rumors today. Yesterday?"

"That High Wizard Talmar was deathly sick. That it started suddenly when he was showing off some wonderful new trick. Some rumors called it livecopper madness, others boasting sickness. I think some said he was already dead, others that it might be a scheme to bring a bigger audience to a special display this fair." Dilys shrugged. "How many people really take rumors seriously? All I knew for sure was that you'd been called to the Scholars' Pavilion."

He frowned. "Surely all that grew from more than Iris coming to fetch me. Too much of it's too accurate. Did they even mention the globe specifically?"

"Some of them. Others said his new technique involved eggs or seeds or tiny thunderstorms. I culled out what I heard, and there must have been a lot I didn't hear. No, it wouldn't all be so nearly accurate."

"Still . . . I don't think the judge would have said very much. Would Mother Vathilda have started spreading a report of boasting sickness already? But she never left the Scholars' Tent until evening. Could the merchant have seen that much so quickly?"

"Merchant?"

"Ulrad. He came to the Scholars' Tent. I think he was going to pay me for the toys he took yesterday, but it was no time to think about trade."

"And Kara? Has she paid you yet? Well," Dilys added when he shook his head, "I'll try to send them around today. Unless you'd rather be left alone?"

He smiled. "Standing there with my arms stretched out and my doorcords untied? They *were* untied when you came?" She nodded, and he went on, "I must have forgotten to tie them because I wanted to be interrupted."

By me, she thought, or by anyone? "Well," she said, "you could tell me what they owe you and I'd try to find them and collect it for you."

"I don't much feel like reckoning it out. One list at a time."

At this hint that he wanted prodding, that he had not meant to close the subject completely a few moments ago, she said, "What list? Something to do with that old memory you were trying to concentrate?"

He wiped his globe with the hem of his tunic. "The skyreaders must have started yesterday's reports. Laderan and Iris. They left the Scholars' Tent early."

"Torinel," said Dilys, "it must be an unpleasant memory, but don't keep teasing yourself with it. Either concentrate and get to the other side of it, or ignore it and we'll get along without its help."

He began to turn his globe again, smearing fresh fingerprints over its surface. "Talmar's First Name-Lengthening. He fell sick that day, too. It was his first great day. I chipped it for him. I had decided—it must have been a year or more before, it felt as if I'd been making the decision all my life—that I wanted to leave magic for crafting. But I'd kept it my secret. I think Mother may have suspected. Well. I took the notion that my younger brother's First Name-Lengthening was the perfect occasion to tell them. I don't know why. Fifteen years old, you can tangle your mind up with a lot of silly ideas at that age. I could have kept my secret a few more days. Or I could have told our mother and father privately that morning, if it had to be that particular day. I think I did try, but we were busy transforming food for Talmar's feast. So I spoke out when we were all together, feasting him. I said something like ...I think I phrased it, 'Well, Talmariak, now you can be the family's only magic-monger this generation, and I can finally go make toys.' Some sentence like that. And he started choking and went on choking."

After a moment, Dilys said, "Anger?"

"How could I have known it'd anger him? If anything, I think I supposed it'd please him. He always loved the study...for seeming more...clever, more powerful." Torin sighed miserably and slumped lower, his forehead resting on the globe in his hands. "Or maybe it wasn't anger. Maybe it was a sudden rush of extra pride at having the family tradition to himself."

Dilys put down the high wizard's globe, moved her cup out of the way, and slid closer to Torin. "Are you sure that was the exact moment he started choking?" She paused, looked at the globe he held against his face, reached out to push his fingers apart for a better view. "Torinel, look!"

He lifted his head and looked. The reflection could only be the festive dinner he had just described. "It's happened again!" His voice was strange. "How?"

Fearing he might smash the globe, Dilys held it and his trembling hands. "Worry about 'how' later. You were trying to get this scene, weren't you? Why?"

"To . . . to study the foods, see what we ate."

"And list them? Then get your tablet. Quick!" She took the globe and held it as close to her eyes as she could without blurring her sight of the tiny dishes. "Goldcobs," she began while Torin fumbled for tablet and writing-point. "Dewmelons. Apricots—or maybe they're citrons. Cherries, I'm sure by the color—they couldn't be small beetroots?"

Eight

SMALL, THIN AND old, though she still refused to wear harvest colors except for a belt braided of brown and orange ribbon, Vathilda looked frail. But Alrathe saw she had already moved all the furniture in the Scholars' Tent.

In its natural state, the furniture consisted of one long, heavy table for banqueting, two much smaller tables and a cupboard for holding food and tableware, and seven chairs. All these pieces and most of the tableware had been lent by crafters; it was an honor, and it increased the ease with which the items could be sold. At larger fairs, folk often paid for such goods without seeing them until they came to cart them home.

Yesterday Vathilda had transformed one of the small tables into the couch for Talmar when he fell sick. This morning she had moved the large table from lengthwise down the center of the tent to crosswise at one end to serve as a stage. She had lifted a small table and the cupboard up to this stage, one piece on either side, to hold magic-mongers' display equipment ready, and she had transformed one chair into steps for mounting the stage. The other small table and two chairs she had arranged in one corner for private showings. Some folk would pay extra to see certain magical feats too dainty to show well in detail on a stage. It could be one of a magic-monger's most profitable (and more tiring) exercises; it was one of Alrathe's own favorite ways to spend moneygems.

Vathilda was hedging the private-display corner with three more chairs when the judge entered the tent. She gave the newcomer a glance, saw who it was, nodded and turned back to her work, transforming one chair into a cupboard with a curtain pole rising from its top.

Vathilda might well give the day's most pebbly interview. Alrathe had decided the best course would be to stand firm but approach her as if her lack of involvement were unquestionable. "Mother Vathilda."

"Child Alrathe." She walked to another chair.

"I come as a judge, on judge's work."

She transformed the second chair into another small cupboard and curtain pole. "Cousin Judge."

"What do you know," said Alrathe, "about an orangestone pendant transformed last night into a citron?"

"Nothing." She moved to the third chair and changed it into a curtain pole and length of curtain. "We were all too busy last night to spend time in silly pranks like that."

"This is the fruit." Alrathe handed it to her.

She squeezed her dry, age-soft fingers around it, opened them almost at once, and dropped it back to the judge's palm. "A citron. Grown a citron from its flower. Shall I harden it into orangestone for you?"

"No." Alrathe pocketed it once more and began to help Vathilda fix natural rods across the curtain poles. "What do you know of the two men each of whom has asked your granddaughter to share his life?"

"I favor the toymaker." Leaving Alrathe to fix the second cross-rod alone, Vathilda started hooking the curtain up on the first. "What little I know of the adventurer suggests he's proud and unsteady. He might flatter the child into supposing herself the most skillful student of her generation."

Whereas, thought the judge, Torin with his self-doubts and excess of unwanted power would keep Sharys humble and safe from boasting sickness? Aloud: "Would you call Valdart unsteady enough to hide his own marriage token for Sharys and accuse his friend of transforming it, in order to discredit the toymaker in her opinion?"

Vathilda snorted. "Unsteady enough, maybe. I shouldn't say, I don't know him that well. But too proud. He'd not suppose he needed trickery to bring him a woman's choice, not that one. Haven't you got that rod tight yet?" She tested it, then started hooking up the last length of curtain. "Now tell me, Cousin Judge, why you're asking. If you're done with being inscrutable for your own judgely reasons."

Alrathe held back a sigh. "Valdart claims that the pendant disappeared from his tent last night and this citron appeared in its place. He accuses Torin of the mischief."

"Charges his old friend, does he?" Vathilda chuckled. "Marriage instinct can tie strange knots in a brain. He might as well accuse Sharys. Well, no one else will believe it of the toymaker, and it ought to show our girl what kind of man she was ready to wed. As for the pendant, someone else slipped in and took it. There's enough folk who coveted the pretty thing."

"The adventurer had one of Talmar's charms on his door. Do charms lose potency when their makers fall sick?"

"Never. Maybe for other reasons, not for that one." Vathilda rubbed her chin. "Likely the charm didn't recognize trade as mischief. Look for someone who had a citron or two and wanted that pendant more."

Thus did the sorceress clip neatly through the problem.

"Would that trade be fair?" asked the judge. "A citron for an orangestone pendant?"

"In some neighborhoods, I fancy. Ask the merchants.

They'd know more about prices than a magicker's charm
would. But be careful how you question 'em, Child
Alrathe."

"Don't doubt the discretion of a grown judge, Cousin
Vathilda," Alrathe replied, for once ignoring her strong
preference for the honorary 'Mother.' "I appreciate that if
this chink in your charms against thievery became a common thought-knot, you'd lose part of your market."

"I doubt it. There's some difference between trade and
outright thievery, Child Alrathe. The one's inconvenient at
worst, the other can bring hunger, thirst, and shivering.
Still, don't noise it about."

"Some people grow strong emotional attachments for
various possessions. Losing such toys, no matter how fair
the unwanted trade, would cause them more pain than mere
inconvenience."

"Let 'em be careful how they show those toys off, then.
As for 'Dart's precious pendant, my granddaughter would
take that citron just as cheerfully for a marriage toy if she
decides to accept one from him. No need to tell him that. If
he can't see it himself, all the more evidence he's not the
mate for her."

Alrathe decided not to discuss Talmar's malady. With
luck, Hilshar and Sharys would provide as much informa-
tion as necessary about the foods for yesterday's dinner.
The judge left the old sorceress transforming tableware into
small props for the afternoon's display of magic.

Either all Vathilda's family and probably Torin as well
were united in pretense, or the citron was natural and the
pendant hidden somewhere else. Vathilda's explanation of
the chink in protective charms against thievery lengthened
the list of possible culprits, for anyone at the fair might
have stumbled into that trade secret. By judge's right,
Alrathe could call for a general search. But that would
disrupt this Amberleaf Fair to the discomfort of the innocent majority, it would spread knowledge of how to cir-
cumvent the charms, and chances were that the culprit

would have time to bury the pendant at first rumor of the
search.

Assuming this was indeed a case of unagreed trade, not
related to Valdart's proposed use of the pendant for a marriage token, certain minds in certain circumstances would
be likelier than others to spy the chink.

Alrathe believed the reason thievery was so common
was that for some generations the idea of private property
had been crumbling away. Ancient records indicated that
long ago folk had considered land a thing which could be
owned, and perhaps this theory was needed and useful if
records didn't exaggerate the incredible numbers of the
race in that era. Within the last five or six generations
custom had still forbidden new individuals to appropriate
vacant houses at will, and even now such buildings as archives, skyreading towers, and in many towns certain
specialized crafthouses like metalsmitheries and well-
provisioned wineshops were sealed when vacant, to be as-
signed by a panel of judges and craft comrades to qualified
claimants. Very slowly, old customs faded with the needs
that had inspired them. Some far future generation might
no longer need private possessions of any kind. Nevertheless, until the concept of thievery perished of itself through
common lack of concern with material goods, judgework
must include correction of individuals who anticipated this
development by appropriating other people's possessions.

Still, Alrathe guessed that those who snatched on impulse due to early stirrings of a new racial thought pattern
were likelier to steal only when the chance came spontane-
ously, like children seeing pretty toys on the showledge at a
moment the toymaker's back was turned. To seek out or
plan opportunities, to walk footpaths at night looking for
loose doorcords, suggested individuals who might have
stolen in any era of the race's development. The present
problem suggested a nimble-minded culprit with a special
desire for Valdart's pendant. Such a mind would realize
that the distinctive piece of jewelry could hardly be worn in
this immediate neighborhood. True, the practice was not

uncommon of keeping lovely thought-focusing toys for private meditation; but would someone who wanted a jewel for that purpose wish to acquire it by thievery or even una-greed trade? Whereas a traveling merchant or ambitious adventurer could plan to resell crafted orangestone and bluemetal elsewhere.

A dozen or more adventurers had come to this Amber-leaf Fair. Many of them intended to winter hereabouts, and the Storyteller's Pavilion offered them a chance to earn a few more moneygems. But because this last fair was small and late, only two fully-styled traveling merchants had de-layed their autumn departure in order to attend. Remem-bering Laderan's comment about how yesterday Valdart had teased one of these two merchants with his pendant, Alrathe decided that Kara was the next logical person to interview.

But Kara was not in her tent, as the judge learned after verifying with three different fairgoers where and which it was. Not in her tent, or suspiciously silent. The doorcords were tied, the charm knotted tightly. Judgework gave Alrathe the privilege to call through closed curtains, but neither the first nor the second call evoked so much as a rustle within.

Unlike many far-traveling merchants, Kara seemed to delight in blending in with local customs. Where others protected their tents with exotic charms from distant places, like badges to announce their calling, Kara used a new charm of Elder Mage Evandisir's making. Alrathe guessed she had bought it in Lyn Forest and would eventu-ally sell it again as part of her trade goods. Meanwhile it protected her property very well without setting her apart in this neighborhood, and no lesser magic-monger should be disgruntled with her for having bought an Elder Mage's charm in preference to anyone else's. Perhaps, in adopting local customs, she interpreted that of knotted doorcords so strictly as to refuse answering even a judge who called in.

But Alrathe doubted it. Some sound of movement

should have signified her annoyance. Probably she was about her business. Alrathe believed that traveling merchants liked to sell off their old goods during a season's early fairs and concentrate during the later fairs on replenishing their stock. Also, they could well find rainy weather more profitably spent buying than selling. Merchants must buy in any case, for it was half their craft. Other folk often needed to be tempted by a ledge of goods displayed in bright sunlight or they might not buy at all, even fairgoing.

Sometime today, High Wizard Talmar's globe should reach once again the hour of yesterday's banquet. Not wanting to miss that, the judge stopped at the toymaker's tent.

A low conversation progressed sporadically inside, but the doorcords were still untied, so Alrathe pulled back the curtain. Torin sat on his traveling chest, bent forward and pressing a globe to his forehead. The storycrafter who delighted in bold embroidery and delicate tales, Dilys, sat cross-legged in front of him, holding a tablet and watching the globe. Even a lifelong celibate could sense shared duality almost palpable, and Alrathe thought, *These two . . . But the toymaker wants Sharys?*

"Is it?" Torin was asking.

"No," Dilys replied. "So far just my own face. Speaking backwards, I think."

"Maybe the emotion needs to be spontaneous." He sighed, lifted his head and raised one hand as if to make Talmar's gestures over the globe, but caught sight of Alrathe and stood. "Cousin Judge."

"Cousin Torin. Cousin Dilys, I think?"

She also had risen to her feet. "I'm glad you remember my name, Cousin Alrathe. I think I've seen you in my audience sometimes?"

"Yes, I've enjoyed your tales at several fairs, when judgework did not intervene." Alrathe looked at Torin. "You've been experimenting with your own globe?"

The toymaker nodded. "I caught his First Name-
Lengthening dinner once. Not quite by accident, but I can't
seem to do it again at will."

"We watched very carefully that once, however." Dilys
handed Alrathe the tablet. "Your list, Cousin. Some of the
food was too small to see very well, but we tried to check
everything against Torinel's memory."

Alrathe opened the tablet. Names of festive foods were
slashed in hasty letters on the right-hand waxboard. The
left-hand board had a list of common foods, many of the
names enclosed in boxlines, some separated by gaps.

"I tried to write the base foods in corresponding spaces
on the left," Torin explained. "I boxed those I'm not sure
about. A lot of them I don't think I ever knew. I'm sorry.
Father and Mother prepared most of the meal."

"This may be a help, nevertheless." Alrathe could have
wished for greater completeness, and the lists might need
rewriting so the user could compare base and transformed
foods at a glance, but clearly the toymaker had done his
best—with the storyteller's assistance. "Can you also mark
which feast foods, if any, were transformed from unusual
bases?"

Torin drew in his breath as if embarrassed. "Most of the
boxes close in usual base foods, Cousin. I made the list
more by common magical practice than true—that is, specific—memory."

"I understand." Alrathe scanned the list, attempting a
preliminary comparison with what foods Sharys had named
earlier this morning beside Talmar's bed. Olives—carrots,
boxed. Whitenuts—parched corn, unboxed. Powderflour
wafers—cabbage leaves, boxed. Citrons . . . "Citrons are
usually transformed from crab apples, then?" asked the
judge.

"Yes."

Sharys had transformed yesterday's from small potatoes. Of that Alrathe was sure. But what base had she
named for yesterday's dewmelons? "And dewmelons are

commonly transformed from small pumpkins," the judge went on, noting Torin's box.

"In late fall. Earlier in the season, from eggplants or redmelons, as I remember. Generally, we—I mean magic-mongers—try to start with as similar a base as possible. Should I have listed them more completely?"

"No. And whitenuts are usually made from something other than parched corn?"

Torin reached for the list. Alrathe gave it over and watched him frown at it. "Yes. Whitenuts—parched corn, that's usual. I didn't box it because I was sure of that transformation. It was one of my own that day. We should have figured out a more complete notation. I have more tablets. Shall I make a better copy?"

Alrathe would prefer to do the copying. Lists were generally more useful when charted by the user. And it seemed little part of judgework to intrude longer on whatever tender tension these two wove between themselves. "Let me take this tablet for now," said the judge, holding out one hand, "while you rest your brain from this particular problem. You might sort your memories of last night. Let me take Talmar's globe, too. It hasn't reached yesterday's dinner yet?"

Torin gave back the tablet and Dilys fetched Talmar's globe. "No," she said, "it still seems to be reflecting the high wizard alone in his tent last night. Better put it in a carrying bag—I imagine it's too big for your pocket?"

"Much too big." Alrathe smiled.

Taking the globe from Dilys, Torin rolled it into a bag and handed it to the judge. Alrathe closed and pocketed the comparatively small tablet, took a firm grip on the bag, exchanged good-byes, and left, closing the doorcurtains carefully on the aura within the tent.

And yet, mused the judge, proceeding toward the scholars' area, perhaps it was nothing else than deep friendship.

* * *

The other traveling merchant, Ulrad with the exotic but overtight garments, was coming out of Merprinel's tent as Alrathe passed.

"Father Judge!" cried the merchant, jumping back as if they had been about to collide. There had in fact been no such danger, and Alrathe looked at the merchant in surprise. Ulrad blushed a little and amended "Mother Magicker?"

"Cousin." Alrathe smiled, climbing above the temptation to add "skyreader," which would probably be the merchant's next guess. "You were correct, however, with 'Judge.'"

"Ah, yes! Of course! Deep red for judges, blue for magic-mongers, purple for skyreaders—hard to tell apart sometimes, you know, when you let your robes fade out."

"Blue, green, silver or gold for scholars of magic," said Alrathe, "in various shades, depending on the degree. But all magic-mongers wear the white star on their left cheek. We simple skyreaders and judges have no such mark, and no such complicated scale of degree."

"Yes, yes. Strange-looking star. Box with two crosslines through it, more like your number six drawn a bit carelessly. Not the way they draw stars in some other far places I've been." The merchant shifted his carrying-bag to one elbow and gestured at some of the embroidered spangles on his fitted overtunic. "Well," he added, taking his bundle back into both arms, "I've just bought some fine mirrors—paid every pebble Sister Mirror-maker priced 'em at, too. A bit expensive, in my judgment, but worth it, worth it. Fine crafting. Now I'd better get 'em back to my own tent, Cousin Judge."

"I was hatching the hope you might drink a cup of hot herbwater in my tent and answer some questions for me, Cousin."

The merchant fussed with his grip on the carrying-bag. "My mirrors, Cousin Judge . . ."

"You'll have only a few extra steps to carry them, and no one will steal them from beneath our chins."

"The path's getting wet. Slippery. Might be hard enough carrying them safe to my own tent already."

"Leave them with Merprinel until the rain stops and the ground dries," Alrathe suggested. A moment ago Ulrad had seemed ready to chat about the different customs of various neighborhoods, and the judge wanted to milk that mood for a list of comparative values, as of orangestone pendants and citrons.

Ulrad changed his grip again. "Short questions, Cousin Judge? Short answers?"

Suspicion was not a tool Alrathe enjoyed using. If Ulrad seemed without reason nervous and fussy, it might be no more than his character, knobbled by who could say what customs in places far distant? Still, if Kara were suspected, so should Ulrad be for many of the same reasons. "Short questions, Cousin," said the judge reassuringly. "Some of the answers may be long, but uncomplicated. I had hoped to ask them of that other traveling merchant this morning, but finding you first, it occurs to me that you may know trade principles equally well. Cousin . . . Ulrad, is it not?"

"Ah—Trade principles? General questions about trade?" By the birdlike puffing of his broad chest, the merchant was not only reassured, but flattered as well. "Yes, yes, I've been rounding these lands eight or ten years longer than that Kara; I fancy I understand general principles ten or twenty years' better. Yes, Ulrad it is."

He shifted his bundle once more so as to rub the dry-charm at his neck, one of his few articles of local costume, before he stepped out from beneath Merprinel's awning into the rain. He neither mentioned his new-purchased mirrors again nor acted on the suggestion of leaving them with honest Merprinel for a while, but carried them very snug in one arm and linked the other in Alrathe's as they walked on to the judge's tent.

Nine

TALMAR SEEMED TO be recovering. There was that much, at least. Torin had been able to see little difference, but Sharys said she could find improvement. She continued as Talmar's chief nurse during the afternoon; as junior magicker she would have attracted the smallest audience to Vathilda's magic show. And yet, the toymaker thought ironically, Sharys would have been less clumsy than I. He was helping gather moneygems to buy Talmar natural comforts for his convalescence. That was some salve for the conscience. Unfortunately, it smeared.

Torin had been starting to tell Dilysin at last of that strange midnight interview with the statue of Ilfting the Dwarf, when Sharys came to his tent. Maybe he should have tied the doorcords upon Dilys and himself, but on a day when news of his brother could come at any moment . . . The storyteller had politely left him alone with the conjurer, knowing his hopes. But Sharys had come only to beg him to sit here all afternoon, in the Scholars' Pavilion, displaying skills he had stopped studying twenty years ago.

Sharys had left, Dilys had not returned, and the toymaker
had spent the rest of the morning in a long failure to com-
pose his thoughts. About midday, feeling no hunger, he
had boxed his globe for safe carrying, filled a bag with
statuettes and other small toys, left his tent with doorcords
knotted about the charm, checked on his brother's condition, visited Alrathe's tent to tell the judge where he would
be and to start Talmar's globe in its backward review once
more, Alrathe having had another chance to study yesterday's banquet.

Then Torin settled into the Scholars' Pavilion with Vathilda, Hilshar, and the two skyreaders. Skyreaders would
not usually help with a magic-mongers' show, but since
this one was for the specific benefit of a suffering fellow
student, Laderan and Iris agreed to collect the audience's
payment.

So far in the alcove for private showings Torin had en-
tertained five buyers, one at a time. They seemed equally
awed by his successes and amused by his clumsiness. As
early afternoon wore on toward middle afternoon and the
toymaker grew better adjusted to the knowledge that they
came to watch a curiosity, he began wishing he had eaten
some lunch after all. He poured a cup of cold water and
transformed it into milk, took a handful of parched corn
and transformed it into nutmeats. When the next buyer was
gone, he would take his few minutes' rest to quit the alcove and get some hot beverage.

The next buyer pushed aside the curtain and came in. It
was Dilys.

She said, "I just passed a little boy with a very little
rabbit—about as big as a prune—and it was alive."

Torin nodded. "Transformed into animation. It'll wear
off sooner or later. I explained that."

"It looked like a rabbit of Torin the toymaker's design."

He nodded again and drank some milk.

She sat and put her hands on the small table between
them.

"Yes," he said, waving at one shelf of the left-hand cupboard, "I charged him a little extra. I brought along some of my toys for the chance of selling them. I sell them for the same prices I would ask anywhere else. The price for transforming them into the appearance of life is included in the small stone the buyers paid to see a private display of the toycrafter half-scholar trying to craft magic." His adjustment to magic-mongering for the afternoon was gone, and he felt ashamed. "The small stone for the private display goes to Talmar. The price for any toys I sell stays in my own pocket. I try to make it clear to the buyers that the toys won't stay alive very long."

Dilys looked toward the pile of nutmeats near Torin's hand, then toward the cupboard shelves. "Do you also do food transformations?"

"Yes."

"Then change a couple of those small potatoes into citr —into little cakes for me. I paid mý small stone. I didn't try to persuade Iris to let me in to see you as a personal visitor."

He chose two potatoes, laid them on the table, put his hand on them and tried to concentrate. One turned into a small cake. The other turned into a citron.

"Well." She scooped them to her side of the table before he could offer to correct the mistake. "Fine. My tongue rather tingled for citrons anyway."

"Better eat them quickly. They might untransform at any time."

"What do I owe for the potatoes?"

He waved his hand in negation.

"If other people pay the usual price for toys," said Dilys, "I assume they also pay the usual price for base foods." She put two large stones on the table.

He picked one up and looked at it with the absorption of a mind trying to avoid more personal thoughts. Plain granite, but the carving, though worn, was as delicate as that generally used on the semi-precious small stones and precious pebbles. A moneygem carver who loved the craft had made this. "Vathilda supplied most of the food," said

Torin. "So she'll get the pay. One stone's enough for the potatoes."

"Then transform something for me to drink. Some red wine."

He poured a cup of water and transformed it. There should be no charge for water, but when Dilysin determined on generosity one needed equal determination to debate it with her. Torin put both stones in Vathilda's box.

Dilys sipped the wine and shook her head. "No. I don't want wine after all. Too depressing in rainy weather. Can you change it into cider? Mild cider."

He complied, wondering if the wine had been sour. He too had noticed how wine could increase melancholy, but was her mood so depressed?

She tasted the cider and nodded. "Much friendlier."

"Your storytelling this afternoon?"

"Went very well, considering. It's surprising how many people came to hear stories when they could have chosen Vathilda's magic show instead."

"And the half-toycrafter—half-conjurer."

"I didn't say that. They could have spent their money-gems to help a sick student, not to enrich a group of preening storytellers. Well, you still have a good-sized audience out there watching Vathilda. Maybe our pavilions will trade audiences about midafternoon."

He picked up a nutmeat and rolled it between thumb and forefinger. "Maybe people sense that your tales are more real than our transformations."

She ate half her citron in one bite. "Then they sense more than I do. Well, I paid a fine moneygem to see some of your display transformations."

He looked at his toys.

"No," she said. "You didn't craft them to come alive. Show me some traditional magickers' skills."

He took another small potato, transformed it successfully into a blue egg, held the egg for three breaths of concentration, and pinched the shell apart. Raw yolk and clear slid out to plop on the table.

"I have a feeling," said Dilys, "that started out right but didn't quite finish as it should have."

"The feat is to transform the egg into a full-grown bird inside the shell. When you break the shell, the bird flutters out."

"And when the transformation unknits?"

"Sometimes, apparently, this one doesn't. When a skillful enough magicker uses real eggs. Or else the bird grows younger. Or changes into the same kind of bird that would have hatched from the natural egg—when a magician hatches a wren from a chicken's egg, for instance. It must be some kind of full-grown bird small enough to fit inside the shell."

"At worst, I suppose the danger of a falling mess isn't that much greater than when natural birds fly overhead." She put the rest of her citron into her mouth.

The toymaker grinned. "Less. The birds flutter out and down to the table. They look fullgrown, but they haven't learned to fly. When wizards and mages do the trick at ceremonies, they put fullgrown flying birds in bags or baskets, transform them into eggs ahead of time, then transform them back into birds. The bags or baskets stay eggshells until after the display. It's a much more complicated trick. Though even the simple magician's version seems to be more than I should have attempted." He touched the raw egg and changed it into a piece of jellied candy, broke it, and offered half to her.

She accepted and started eating it at once. "Mm. Very tasty. Lemon?"

"I'd meant to flavor it saffron."

"Well, I've just had citron on my tongue. The person who refined a high wizard's new globe technique this morning calls a magician's trick too complicated now?"

He shrugged. "Power half-trained."

She started to say something, stopped, and ate the small cake before it turned back into a potato.

Torin was not sure why he had brought the marriage toy Shrays refused yesterday. Perhaps some lingering hope, or some reluctance to leave it guarded only by a charm when another marriage toy had disappeared last night from Valdart's similarly charm-protected tent. He had not unpacked it. He had tucked it, rolled in the large carrying-bag, into the back corner of the cupboard's lowest shelf.

"I know I have power for magicking," he went on. "From both my parents, I suppose. It may seem wasteful not to use it. But crafting is a kind of working with transformations, too. Transformations that don't unknit themselves. When you find you have two skills . . ." He paused. The thought began to sound vainglorious.

But she quietly finished it for him. "And only time in your life to concentrate on one skill, how can you choose, if not by what you most want to do."

"Some poets say the more perfect path upwards is the one you like least."

"Some poets climb in a fog. You need some happiness to keep you climbing."

He reached down for the carrying-bag, extracted the marriage toy, laid it on the table and slipped the pair of figures from their own small, padded bag.

She looked at them and shook her head. "No. Don't animate those. Don't craft magic on them."

"I wasn't going to. They've already been transformed by simple craftwork. From a length of cherrywood." He slid them across the table to her. "Dilysin. How would you add a fourth syllable?"

She picked the figures up and moved them carefully as far as they would go. "They don't come apart, do they? There's no way of taking them apart without breaking them. Was that the way you carved them, or did it happen yesterday when you accidentally brought them to life?"

"It's the way I carved them. From a single length." He held the little padded bag out to her.

She considered it for a moment, as if she were feeling his thoughts. Then she took it, slipped the marriage toy inside, pulled the drawstrings tight and handed it back to him. "Sharys has first refusal."

"I think she's already given it."

"You persuaded her to save her decision until the end of this fair." The storyteller drank off the rest of her cider, swallowed hard, and blinked. "She might still show a few measures of good sense by tomorrow evening." She stood. "And I think—I think you should wait that long before making your own decisions, Torin. Either of them." She turned and left like a person hurrying across cracking ice.

Torin rested his face in his hands. His elbow scattered nutmeats that were turning back into parched corn, but fortunately missed his cup of watery milk. He wondered if he should tell them, Iris and Vathilda and the others, that he wanted an hour's respite, or even that he wanted to stop playing at magic-craft for moneygems. But he knew he would stay. Even if it were not for his brother's better comfort, he could hardly hope to make a decision for the rest of his life if he could not keep to what he had decided for a single rainy afternoon.

Alrathe was studying the recopied food lists when brisk footsteps stopped outside the tent and a low-pitched, vaguely familiar voice said, "Cousin Judge?"

"My cords are unknotted."

The newcomer entered, thin, tall, and dressed well but plainly, the costume's only adornment being a line of yellow starbursts embroidered round the hem of the russet-brown festival cape. The clothing was almost over-typical for this neighborhood, as if the wearer tried too ardently to be anonymous in a crowd of individuals. Yet this person was memorable, not so much for any single remarkable feature as for the way they fit together. Other folk were so tall they had to stoop on entering tents, had equally dark skin, black hair silvering in streaks, slight indentations between cheekbones and jawline, shrewd but inward-looking eyes with perfect, blue-tinged whites. Other folk carried their bodies with equal poise and spoke with equally low-

pitched, quiet voices. But few of these other folk seemed
to wear all their traits like garments they might someday
choose to change at will.

"I find it prudent always to call in, whether cords hang
knotted or loose," the newcomer remarked. "They say you
came to my tent this morning looking for me."

"Merchant Kara, is it? You're not misinformed."

"Do you suspect me of stealing Valdart's orangestone
and bluemetal token last night, Cousin Judge?"

"Perhaps," said Alrathe, meeting candor with candor.
"How did you hear of that theft?"

She shrugged. "Rumors."

"Indeed? I have said nothing except to individuals
known to be closely concerned, either with the trouble or
with one another. I'd have trusted their discretion. Which
of them has bleated, I wonder?"

"I don't know. Valdart, I'd not be surprised. I have no
special reason to protect whoever, but I heard it from Kasdan the meal-merchant, Elvar the music-crafter, and a child
who wears the name, I think, of Ond. I doubt any of them
is closely concerned. Elvar and the child also told me of
your visit. May I sit?"

Alrathe nodded, and Kara sat on a cushion, folding her
long legs gracefully.

"If you cannot tell me the source of the rumors you
heard," said the judge, "perhaps you can repeat their substance."

"I have a short memory for rumors, Cousin Judge. I
ignore whatever does not stir my own plans. They said
Valdart's pendant was stolen and gone. I meant to learn the
truth or exaggeration of that from the adventurer himself
this afternoon, because I had still hoped to buy the thing
from him. What other details my three gossips added
sieved through my brain without staining the mind-mesh."

"Then they did not hint that I might suspect you?"

"I believe the music-crafter grinned."

Alrathe could well imagine that Elvar's grin, coupled
with news of a judge's visit, might raise apprehensive spec-

ulations. So, however, might awareness of guilt. "Elvar music-crafter," said the judge, "seems fond of pretending to think the worst of everyone. But I did not mention this business of Valdart's orangestone when I asked which was your tent. If Elvar or young Ond coupled the two things, they did so in their own minds."

"Then you want to question me about something else?" said Kara with no visible release of tension. But she had brought no visible tension with her, only relaxed wariness. If her explanation of rumors had been hastily devised to cover a nervous mistake, she seemed unlikely to slip a second time.

Alrathe sighed. Judges' authority was limited over travelers born elsewhere, particularly travelers like this one. "Merchant Kara, we'll sing no over-complicated duets. If I suspect you, it's less on account of your actions than on account of your simple presence here."

"I see. Elvar's mind coupled the two things with some logic."

"Eager logic, however," said the judge.

"Am I suspected as one of many fairgoers, or as a stranger who visits your neighborhood one year in three?"

"Both. I suspect you because you're a fairgoer here, but I seek you out early because you're a strange traveling merchant."

"And eventually you may work down to the local music-crafter." Kara nodded. "But I always understood that your magic-mongers' charms, knotted across a door, kept out any meddler except perhaps other magic-mongers, and that they are professionally loathe to meddle. Tell me if I've understood imperfectly. I left my own stock protected with such a charm."

"The circumstances of Valdart's pendant appear to be far from typical of our neighborhood. Your property should be safe."

"We'll hope so, or I may have my own case to bring you." The merchant stood. "Meanwhile, I lose trading time. I dislike paying for nothing, but if there's no other way to settle this, I'll hand over what would have been a fair price for that piece of jewelry. Rather than leave your neighborhood under a tarnish of suspicion and perhaps return in three years to find it still heavy over my repute."

Alrathe rose and put the small kettle of water on the brazier. "Our local customs require host to offer guest refreshment, whatever the reason for the visit. Besides, we haven't reached the first questions I wanted to ask you."

Kara raised one eyebrow and glanced at the kettle. "I'll stay to answer your questions, but I'd prefer cool wine to hot tea."

"I have no wine. Cherry cordial?"

Kara turned her right palm up in what was clearly a gesture of assent, though seldom used hereabouts. She waited until Alrathe had poured a small cup of cordial and put it into her hand before she spoke again. "Your questions, Cousin Judge?"

"By coincidence, they concern the fair prices of orange-stone pendants, among other goods brought here from far away, such as citrons."

"By coincidence," Kara repeated, raising her eyebrow again.

And perhaps, thought the judge, by some providential economy of effort. Kara, if anyone, could have entered Valdart's tent and exchanged citron for pendant smoothly while he slept. It was a temptation to accept her offered reimbursement without further probing, as implied confession combined with immediate correction. But if Kara were not guilty, it would be unjust to her, no matter how seemingly gentle a solution—unjust also to the true culprit, who would go uncorrected. And clues to other problems might hinge on the answer to this one. So Alrathe must avoid the temptation.

Ten

WHEN DILYS LEFT the Scholars' Pavilion, she walked purposefully through the fairgrounds into the woods, sat down in the partial shelter of a huge old uprooted oak tree, and emptied herself of tears.

"I should have accepted his token," she said half aloud. "I should have accepted it and let that little fool Sharys scrabble for someone else."

But how well would we fit together? she wondered. Aye, as friends . . . we're good friends. I think I've become a better friend to him than Valdart, no matter what friends they may have been as children. But Torinel mild and me temperish? As mated parents? With my hard edges? How well would we really fit each other?

She remembered the feel of those carved cherrywood figures so vividly that when she glanced down she saw her hands twitching as if they still played with the linkage. "His marriage toy," she whispered again. "I should have accepted it when I had the chance."

For some moments longer she sat, hearing the rain and

examining possible futures as if she were crafting tales.
Torinel as toycrafter, Torinel as magicker and high mage.
She herself always as storyteller, but here helping turn
wood as it seasoned, there dabbling in simple conjurers'
tricks to amuse their children. Always there were children,
usually two, sometimes one. And when these offspring
were grown—she calculated how old they would be then,
she and Torin, and found they should still have time to
adventure for a few years, like his mother, if they chose.
And at last to lie down somewhere beneath a great tree that
would drop its seeds into the compost of their bodies. Or to
put on harvest colors and settle again in their two neighboring cottages. Always there were two cottages in her daydreams, with a third and fourth for the children as they
grew old enough. Most families found it the smoothest way
of living together, since time to be alone had always been
among life's essentials. It would be all the more essential
for Torin and Dilys, accustomed as they both were to fashion their craft materials in private, and determined as she
was not to interfere with this choice he must remake,
whether to craft toys or study magic.

Yes, she thought, stubborn-edged as I am and soft as
young Sharys may look—would she live content with a
crafter? Or would she try urging him back to magic? So I
might be more tolerant with him, after all!

But if the young conjurer has more ambition than to
tolerate a crafter, why is she about to accept an adventurer?
And am I not trying to push him back toward toycrafting,
whether I mean to or not? Maybe she thinks she wants
Valdart because one hardly need feel much concern either
way with the rank and syllables a man can earn who is
absent most of the time.

But I'm not a judge. And I'm trying to study real minds
as I study the little people in my tales. Unjust. Unjust to
them . . . maybe even to myself.

She sighed and blinked, but only a few more tears
squeezed out. She was tired of crying, and in four or five
hours she would have to climb the platform in the Story-

tellers' Pavilion again for her evening session. She should have put on her drycharm before wandering about this afternoon. Despite the old fallen tree around her, her cloak was rain-wetted through, her hair and tunic damp to the skin. She got up, brushed off mud and leaf-crumbs as well as she could, and returned to her tent.

Shedding her clothes, she cocooned herself in bed and tried to nap, but quickly decided she was too restless. Her body would not cool (so that the blanket felt overwarm), her mind would not stop darting between Torin and tonight's stories, and her throat scratched. She hoped that last was imagination. She had worn her throat-charm, but sometimes hard weeping seemed to cancel out protective magic against chill and phlegm.

Kasdan the mealcrafter made an excellent, soothing posset of scalded milk, honey, strong brandy, and blended spices. That, with a plate of melted cheese, toasted bread, and candied fruit, was a prospect she could use to help her forget other things for half an hour. She rose and dressed in dry clothes. Her long cloak still wet, she had only her short autumn festival cape for outer wear, so she put on both spare tunics for added warmth.

Though this time she wore drycharm as well as throat disk, the day seemed chillier than she had noticed before, and she almost wished she had folded her blanket round her shoulders for a makeshift cloak, never mind how it looked. Fortunately, Kasdan had several braziers aglow in his small meal pavilion, and space was clear beside one of them. She told the mealcrafter what she wanted, paid for it, and settled down on the cushions, closing her eyes while she waited.

Kasdan had eight or nine other buyers besides Dilys, a decent crowd for so small a fair at an hour midway between common mealtimes. The weather was helping his custom, too. Populated mealshops did not tend to be the quietest places on rainy afternoons when folk liked to feel some need for warming liquors to supplement their protective charms. Several of this group seemed also to be feel-

ing some need for loud voices, so Dilys thought it as well
they had chosen Kasdan's pavilion rather than the Storytellers' or Scholars'.

Listening to other people's conversations was a recom-
mended tool of storycrafting, and more than one of these
conversations was certainly loud enough to overhear with
no rude strain. But in trying to sort one dialogue from
another perhaps she dozed, for suddenly she realized that
someone was repeating her name. She opened her eyes and
saw Valdart standing above her.

"That's right, Senior Storyteller." He grinned. "Thought
you were ignoring me."

She shook her head. "Only drowsing. Your session's
over? How did it go?"

"Heavy enough." He hoisted a small bag, pinching it to
make the moneygems grind audibly within. "Aye, Storycrafter, I should be able to buy pretty Sharys another marriage token before tomorrow. Maybe not so fine as that
orangestone, but it's me she'll be accepting. The token's
just a symbol, after all."

"Don't buy it from Torin."

"From Tor? Not likely. You're welcome to his whole
stock. Well, Sister, I'll leave you to your drowse."

He turned away and she sighed in relief. Conversation
with Valdart was not her idea of restful pastime, especially
under present circumstances. But he seemed sincere in his
grudge against the toymaker. She wondered, for Torin's
sake, whether this crack in their old friendship could ever
mend, whether Valdart would come to believe Torin's innocence if no proof appeared. And she wondered if what
she felt was so visible that Valdart had consciously teased
her in welcoming her to Torin's whole stock, or whether he
had simply used a rhetorical "you."

As she wondered, she heard him buy a cup of wine and
begin a conversation with someone behind her.

"Well, merchant," said the adventurer, and Dilys
thought she heard him grind his moneygems in their pouch
again.

"Well, adventurer? I . . . er . . . fear I'm not sure of your name."

"You knew it well enough last fair. Trying to buy my last piece of beyond-ocean orangestone."

"Orangestone?"

"My pendant. Your memory's crumbly, Brother. I hope you keep careful lists of your own stock."

"Ah, yes, yes!" said the merchant, whose voice Dilys had not yet quite connected with a face. "Orangestone and bluemetal. Nicely crafted. That was what I fancied most, not the stone."

"Fancied? Came near tangling your tongue to buy it."

"Yes. Well, strange coincidence, I found another fellow with one much like it. Anxious to sell it between fairs, he was. Now I think of it, could be two halves of a walnut with that one you had. The metalwork, at least. I can't answer for the stone. Very common stuff beyond the ocean, I understand."

"Not common here. You were lucky to find that other fellow, Brother. Anyone I might have shipped with?"

A pause, as if the merchant shrugged before he spoke again. "Tallish fellow. Strong shoulders."

"No, not much memory for names, have you? Well, just as well you bought his when you had the chance. Mine's gone, if you hadn't heard. Not that I'd have sold it anyway."

"Oh? Should've sold it to me, then. Ah—How gone?"

"Stolen. Or transformed, might as well be stolen."

How stubborn-foolish that adventurer is, thought Dilys. Magical transformations unknit. If his citron stays a citron, he should know Torin's not responsible.

But such proof might be long in appearing. One of Torinel's accidental transformations into life, a little brook-stone turtle, had crawled around his workship for five days before unanimating itself, until they feared it might feel hunger and thirst. That had stirred up one of their first long conversations about the rightness of changing such accidental transformations back at once.

Meanwhile, here in Kasdan's pavilion, Valdart was saying, "Well, Brother, bring out this twin pendant and maybe
I'll buy it from you." Again Dilys thought she heard his
moneygems. She could picture him kneading the pouch
with his thick, brown fingers.

"I . . . uh . . . don't have it with me."

"Left it in your tent with a charm-neutering magicker on
the prowl around this fair? Overtrusting of you, Brother
Merchant."

Dilys felt her breath hotten.

"Well, I only heard rumors a little while ago," the merchant was saying.

"And you sit here with your cup of wine, Brother?
Come on, let's get back to your tent and check your stock
against your list."

"I'm sure it's all safe. Charms all around—two on my
door and another on every chest."

"And I tell you I had one of High Wizard Talmar's own
on my door." Valdart must have drunk Kasdan's strong
wine too fast. His speech was already slurring a little.

"They say High Wizard Talmar's on his deathbed. So
his charms could be . . . uh . . . coming undone."

Valdart snorted. "Not likely!"

"Well, their transformations hereabout . . . Besides, the
charms on my chests were fashioned by the mages of
Thrak and Erbolis," said the merchant.

"I've traveled farther south than Thrak and farther north
than Erbolis. Aye, and twenty days into the land beyond
the western ocean. And charms always work best in their
own neighborhoods. And it's one blamed crafty magicker
we've got hereabout watching for chances. Besides, I
want to buy that little bit of bluemetal and orangestone
from you."

"I'm not offering it for sale! Not here. Not yet. It'd be
lost profit. I have to take it at least as far as Weltergrise."

"Tell me what you'd ask for it there."

"Eat two plates of something before you drink any
more, Brother Adventurer," said the merchant.

"Ah? I don't see any plate beside your cup, Brother Merchant. Come on, let's at least take our look at your orangestone and be sure that culprit hasn't found it yet, the way he found mine."

The merchant made some further sound of protest, which was swallowed in the noises of two men getting to their feet, one seemingly pulled.

Dilys breathed slowly and deeply. She might have succeeded in keeping quiet until they had left Kasdan's pavilion. But Valdart's foot hit her thigh in passing, and he halted to give some apology.

"Not much footpath space in here, Senior Storycrafter," he began. "No rudeness meant—"

"Not to me, I suppose." Dilys stood, swinging around into his way, hands on her hips. "You meant enough rudeness to your old friend."

"What?"

"'Culprit.' 'Charm-neutering magicker on the prowl.' 'Blamed crafty magicker.'"

Valdart reddened. "Well, my orangestone's gone, and who else could have done it? Except some blamed charm-neutering magicker?"

"But you meant Torin, didn't you? Your old friend! Fragile friendship on your part, not even to trust—"

"Here, here, gently," the merchant tried to interpose.

"All right, I meant Torin," said Valdart. "Blamed fragile friendship on his part, too, and he strained it first. And if you want to think maybe I stepped on you just now because of him—"

"It was the wine treading down," said the merchant. "The wine shaking his steps, Sister."

"I guessed that much." Dilys glanced around at the eight or nine other buyers and Kasdan, standing with her meal in his hands, all watching the wine-brawl. A good number for this time of day, but the tent could hold four times as many. "It certainly wasn't the press of the crowd. But even supposing the worst, Adventurer," she went on, lowering her voice, "even supposing Torin was the one who took your

silly orangestone—I don't believe it, but pretend he did—
not even you can be so foolish as to think he'd do it for the
thing's value in moneygems, so you have no reason to suggest anyone else's property is under threat!"

"But if it wasn't your toymaker," said the merchant,
who suddenly seemed eager to get out of Kasdan's tent, "if
some thief is on the prowl with a charm-neutering trick—"

Dilys looked from Valdart to the merchant. "Far-
traveler. Yes. You bought quite a number of toys from
Torin yesterday. Two bagsful, as I remember. Ulrad, isn't
it? You were going to bring round your payment this morning."

"Aye—aye . . ." He shook his head. "I didn't? Razors!
You're sure?"

"I was with him most of the morning."

"Ah . . . ah . . . Pure oversight. Here—" Ulrad lifted his
money pouch. "I'll pay you now. For him."

"If I knew his prices, you'd have paid me yesterday
before I let you carry those toys away." Dilys took hold of
Ulrad's arm. "He's spending this afternoon in the Scholars'
Pavilion, if you hadn't heard. We can go there right now.
Don't worry, with your business they'll let you in to see
him without making you pay for his little magic show."

"Later!" Valdart clamped his hand on Ulrad's right
shoulder. "I've got my own business with this merchant
first. He can find his way to the magickers' tent afterwards."

Still gripping Ulrad's arm, Dilys put her other hand on
Valdart's and started straining to lift it away.

The merchant gasped and tried to pull free of them both,
but they were all too closely interlinked by now—like
Torin's figures, Dilys thought vaguely, but different. She
was half aware of shouts and people hurrying forward to
separate the brawlers, but before anyone could reach them
they had toppled over. The brazier fell, hot coals rolling
out on the rugs, and people who had come to pull the
brawlers apart turned their attention to stamping out
smoulders instead.

Kasdan deliberately used Dilys' milk-posset to quench a cushion that was smoking with several embers. She did not try to see what he had done with her plate of food. She squashed a last coal, leaving her foot on it slightly too long and snatching it away with a gasp. She looked around the floor, but all danger of fire seemed to have been washed and trampled away.

"Well!" said the mealseller.

"Not my fault!" said Ulrad. "It's not my fault. Everyone here could see—"

"Damages to my rugs, cushions, and floor matting," Kasdan went on, studying the scorchmarks and winestains, "at least twenty pebbles' worth."

"The merchant's justified," Dilys admitted, though it hurt a little. "He was not responsible." She glanced at Valdart. "But this adventurer deserves to help pay for your damages!"

Valdart folded his arms across his chest and returned her stare. "We weren't the ones who stood up in your way when you tried to leave the tent, Senior Storyteller."

"Either I'll have twenty pebbles before any of you leave my pavilion," the mealcrafter said quietly, "or I'll take my grievance to the judge against all three of you."

Dilys folded her arms in imitation of Valdart. "All right. Let's go to the judge now. All of us." But—twenty pebbles? So much? And her foot burned like the coal she had stamped, and she had brawled like a wine-fool, without even the fumes in her brain to explain it. And her throat definitely scratched when she swallowed. Someday all this might help add texture to her tales, but it was very uncomfortable right now. And the report might swell her audiences for the rest of the fair, but she wished she would not need to face them.

Eleven

"So," said Alrathe, "in coastal towns beyond the western ocean such a bluemetal and orangestone pendant might sell for as little as one of our large stones, which is the equivalent price of a single citron in Weltergrise during their harvest season."

Having drunk the last of her cordial, Kara turned the cup in her long fingers. "I have never myself been beyond the ocean. I've only heard adventurers boasting they had bought such jewelry for a large stone or two. Also, Brother Ulrad has spoken loosely of such equivalent values. I assume he's heard similar travelers' boasts."

"Then in theory some neighborhood might exist where such a pendant and a single citron would bring identical prices."

Kara shrugged. "Aye, but I'd guess that neighborhood would have to exist in the middle of the western ocean. They say there are islands, of course. Remember, too, that folk beyond the ocean might value your common large stones more highly than you'd think, for their fine carving and rarity in those neighborhoods."

"Well, I see, Cousin Kara, that for complexity of number-knotting your merchantcraft must be as interesting as our skyreaders' study."

"And now you'll want an account of my actions?"

Alrathe nodded, though suspecting Kara's account would offer little evidence in either direction.

"Well, then. Yesterday morning, after seeing to my pack animals in the enclosure, I purchased goods from Merprinel the mirror-maker and Camys the weaver. In the afternoon I visited the toymaker—by chance, at the same time Brother Ulrad was there. We made our selections, but could not pay because Torin was called to his brother the wizard's bedside and those who came to watch his showledge, first the young skyreader and later Dilys the storyteller, did not know his prices. After Torin, I visited my animals again. After seeing them fed, I ate in Kasdan's meal tent. As I had at midday. In the evening I listened to a couple of storytellers, Dilys and Valdart, then returned to my own tent, packed my day's purchases, and slept. This morning after visiting the animal enclosure I went to pay Torin for yesterday's purchases, but I heard a conversation within and guessed his doorcords hung loose by oversight. I traded with Boken the furniture crafter, bought another meal from Kasdan, and visited Elvar the music-crafter. Elvar did not mention that you had come looking for me until after he sold me as many of his instruments as I chose to purchase. The child gave me the same message in passing when I was already on my way to you. I can gather witnesses for my movements in the daytime and evening, but not for the hours I was alone last night, and I suppose they interest you most."

Alrathe nodded again. If Kara had slipped into Valdart's tent last night and exchanged citron for orangestone, she would not likely confess it. "The amount of time you must have spent with the furniture crafter surprises me. I'd have thought furniture too bulky for traveling merchants' stock."

"With furniture makers, I trade in scraps of wood for inlay work." Kara shifted slightly. It seemed a calculated rather than a restless motion. "If I have answered your questions for the present, Cousin Judge, I would like to pay the toymaker. I understand he's giving displays of magic in the Scholars' Tent. And visit my animals before supper. I had meant to purchase from your shoemaker this afternoon, but now that must probably wait until tomorrow."

"You show great care for your animals."

"Far-traveling merchants can recover losses of stock more easily than losses of good animals to carry it. At present I have only two adventurers in my employ, and they share the task of watching my donkeys and mules. Derek I can trust, but I have some doubts of Vittor."

Alrathe lifted one hand in a gesture of good-bye. "Prosper in your trading, Merchant. Should I want to speak with you again, I'll send someone to find you."

Kara rose. "You may search my chests, but had I stolen Valdart's pendant I would of course have buried it in the woods, to recover secretly after the fair."

The judge had so reasoned and therefore made no search plans, but Kara's quiet offer might be a ruse to forestall searching. If that were her intent, however, would she not have made the remark earlier in this interview? As Alrathe quickly rethought the decision not to search, Kara lifted the doorcurtain and looked out, then stepped back into the tent.

"Four people are coming," she said. "They've just passed the Scholars' Pavilion, and they have the look of a group in need of judgework." She smiled. "One of them is my fellow travelling merchant, Brother Ulrad."

"Did you recognize the others?"

She glanced out again. "Dilys the storyteller, Valdart the adventurer, Kasdan the meal-merchant. A wine brawl, I'd guess."

"Dilys? You're sure?"

Kara shrugged. "They're almost here, Cousin Judge."

Their footsteps were audible now, through the gentle rain. Alrathe sighed. Continued freedom from other judge-craft had been too much to hope, even at a fair as small as

East'dek's, but perhaps this new problem would be simple and easily judged. "You may go about your own business at will, Cousin Kara."

She nodded and pulled back the doorcurtain, standing to one side. Dilys entered first, looking curiously and perhaps a little suspiciously at the merchant. Valdart and Ulrad followed, with the mealcrafter last as if herding them all inside.

"Is there one chief complainant," the judge asked them, "or have you all interlinked grievances?"

"I have none!" said Ulrad. "I only want to pay my share and go back to my own business, Parent Judge."

"Don't be fuzz-minded," said Dilys. "You can probably make your own complaint against 'Dart and me and pay nothing."

"All the damage was to my property, Cousin Judge," Kasdan put in. "So I'm chief complainant. If these wine-brawlers want to settle who pays by complaining against one another, that's agreeable to me as long as I have my repayment by nightspread."

Alrathe studied them. Kasdan was sober, as befitted merchants who sold wine. Dilys also looked sober, though angry and ashamed. Valdart seemed tipsy; his face was flushed and he stood grinning cockily, with hands on hips and chest puffed out. Ulrad was pale and looked as if he were swaying a little, but whether from drink or nervousness would be difficult to say at a glance.

"I'll interview Kasdan first," the judge decided, "Dilys second, Valdart third, and Ulrad last. I will give a final judgment in Kasdan's pavilion tomorrow morning before breakfast. Cousin Mealcrafter, one night's wait for your payment should not inconvenience you overmuch, now the damage is done."

Kara stepped into the doorway, but paused when Ulrad —not Kasdan—protested.

"My tradecraft, Parent Judge!" said Ulrad. "Good Brother Kasdan asks twenty pebbles. I'll pay my share— seven pebbles, that's even a little more than a third—but

I'll lose more than that in trade if I lose the rest of my afternoon."

"Brother Ulrad has a point," said Kara, though she cocked an eyebrow as if to ask how much trade could be accomplished in the remainder of the afternoon. "Have you made your purchases from Kendys shoemaker yet, Ulrad? I'm willing to take him there with me now, Cousin Judge, and return him here in an hour. I can pay the toymaker what I owe him," she added, looking at Dilys, "and do my other tasks in the evening."

The thought crossed Alrathe's mind that these two traveling merchants could conceivably have stolen Valdart's pendant together. But only one could keep it, they followed different trade routes, they did not appear fully to trust one another, and this wine brawl was not likely to have been part of any preconcerted scheme. "Your offer's generous, Cousin Kara," said the judge. "I agree."

Kara took Ulrad's arm and led him from the tent.

Alrathe fetched out two judges' token. "Dilys, Valdart, you can wait in the Scholars' Tent. Hand these to the place-sellers and they'll let you wait without paying for the magic show."

"I'd rather wait outside in the rain, Cousin Judge," said Dilys.

"And I'd rather wait where it's warm and dry and there's a little entertainment," said Valdart.

"And a chance of insulting your old friend to his ears?" the storycrafter replied.

"Go to the Scholars' Tent," said Alrathe. "If Vathilda or Laderan gives permission, you may wait in one of their tents. But you may not wait outside mine to overhear another's private interview."

The judge spoke with authority. They nodded and left. Dilys limped a little.

Kasdan's complaint was soon made. Alrathe, with half a cup of sweetblend remaining (herbwater was the strongest beverage judges should drink while engaged in their work), made the meal-merchant his choice of plain tea, and Kasdan finished his tale before his cup. He had heard only snatches of the angry conversation, not enough to describe it—let the brawlers tell that story. All he could testify was that the three of them had grabbed each other and fallen in the strain, toppling a good brazier and so causing considerable damage to rugs, cushions, and floormat.

"But your initial figure of twenty pebbles was a hasty estimate?" said the judge at last.

Kasdan drained his cup. "Hasty, but I know my property. I won't be mistaken by more than a pebble or two either way. Depending on how badly that brazier may be knocked askew."

"Go back and make your careful tally of the damage. Then enlist Camys or Boken to make a separate, uninfluenced estimate. You will have your payment when I can be sure how much is fair."

"There's also my loss of time, and the trouble and inconvenience. This wine-brawling always hurts us honest shopcrafters most. Just collecting payment for damages doesn't seem like sharp enough correction to keep it from happening again."

"How many wine brawls have you suffered this season?" asked the judge.

"One during the Horodek fair. That was in my town shop, and they cracked a table leg. Now this one. I know three other mealcrafters who've had to sweep brawlers out of their shops this year to avoid damage."

"Most callings have their hazards. For magic-mongers, it's livecopper madness. For you who sell wine, it's brawling among your buyers. In addition to paying your damages, they shall also pay for my judgment, saving you that cost. Were I to charge them any sharper correction, who could rightly receive the extra moneygems?"

"Aye. Well." Kasdan rose and handed his cup back to Alrathe. "But about waiting till morning for my money. I'd hoped to send round to Boken and Camys and Arlys or Tambur and start replacing things tonight."

"Crafters can be persuaded to wait a day for their payment." Alrathe held out another judges' token. "If they question it, show this as pledge that my judgment tomorrow will assign you fair payment."

Kasdan accepted the disk and bowed politely.

"On your way back to your pavilion," said the judge, "kindly pause at the skyreaders' tent, or Mother Vathilda's, or the Scholars' Pavilion, wherever you find Dilys, and send her to me."

"Cousin Judge." Kasdan nodded and left.

"I'm not sure how it happened," said the storyteller. "I mean, why it happened. . . . Well, in a way I understand it, but . . ."

"Sweet herbwater, savoury, or plain?" said Alrathe.

"Sweet. Sincerest thanks, Cousin Judge."

Alrathe dropped an extra pinch of blend into the cup. The kettle had never been long off the brazier since Kara's visit.

"I can pour it myself, Cousin Judge," said Dilys. Alrathe let her. "And you?" she added.

Alrathe answered with a headshake and two fingers laid atop the cup that still contained a little tea, now long cool, infused during the interview with Kara. "In what way do you understand how it happened?"

Dilys sat and curled her fingers around her cup. "Valdart had been speaking harshly of Torin, as much as accusing him to the merchant—not by name, but . . . Well, I knew who he meant, and it made my breath ragged. Then he started out with the merchant. I don't think the merchant really wanted to go, but Valdart insisted they had to tally his stock, and besides, Valdart wanted to buy a pendant the merchant was boasting about, another orangestone and bluemetal piece to replace the one he claims Torin transformed. Valdart's foot hit my leg on their way out. I suppose it was accidental, but I . . . felt like tinder and his foot was the spark. So I jumped up and accused him of blaming his old friend without evidence. The merchant tried to soothe us. But I remembered he still hadn't paid Torin for the toys he took away yesterday. I felt hungry and achy, and I started insisting the merchant come to the Scholars' Pavilion and pay Torinel at once. Valdart insisted he had first claim on the merchant's afternoon. We both took hold of the merchant, as if we could pull him to one place or the other, and that's how we tangled together and all toppled over." She sipped her steaming herbwater. "Oh, that soothes the throat a little. I'd bought one of Kasdan's milk possets, but he used it to dowse a burning cushion. Not that it wasn't his right—I'm not asking for my moneygem returned—but I don't imagine I'll dare go back to his pavilion and buy another posset today. Well. We did stop brawling as soon as we realized the damage, when we all got up and helped stamp out the little fires. That's how I burned my foot." She grinned ashamedly.

"Have you asked the magic-mongers for some salve?"

"Not yet."

"Do so as soon as you leave me. Cousin Hilshar might be the most sympathetic."

Dilys nodded and drank more tea.

"But by your own account, no brawl would have occurred if you had not tried to delay Valdart and Ulrad from leaving."

She sighed and bent her head over her cup. Alrathe thought she was crying. She said with obvious effort, "Well, if I have to pay it all, I will. But it doesn't seem fair for that cocksure fragile 'old friend.' Couldn't you at least correct him for spreading that kind of talk about 'sneaky magickers'?"

"Can you repeat more exactly what they said?"

She unpocketed her handycloth, wiped her cheeks and blew her nose, tilted her head back and closed her eyes. "Valdart started by greeting the merchant. Ulrad didn't recognize him at first, but 'Dart reminded him he'd tried to buy that ugly orangestone pendant a few fairs ago. Then Valdart added it had been stolen or transformed last night. Ulrad said in that case 'Dart should have sold it to him.

That was when the adventurer talked a lot about 'some untrusty magicker on the prowl around this fair,' and started urging Ulrad to go back to his tent and make sure his own stock was safe. Ulrad protested that he had two or three charms in his doorcords and another on every chest, and they were from far distant neighborhoods, but 'Dart answered that charms work best where they're made and weaken with distance. 'Dart pointed out that his own tent was guarded by one of High Wizard Talmar's charms, Ulrad theorized that it might be weakening now with Talmar's health, and 'Dart replied that made no difference hereabouts. Oh, and somewhere in all that was when Ulrad boasted about buying another bluemetal and orangestone pendant almost identical to the one 'Dart was showing off, from another adventurer between fairs. I suppose Valdart wanted to buy this new one so he could offer it to Sharys in place of the other. Ulrad didn't want to sell, but 'Dart sounded determined." Eyes still closed, she grinned. "It may make a rare scene if 'Dart ever does get into Ulrad's tent and start bullying him to see the thing."

"So the merchant had not wanted to leave Kasdan's pavilion with the adventurer."

"No. He walked along quietly enough, but I'm sure he didn't want to go. Not until I stood and blocked their way, and then he only wanted to smooth matters and get out of the tent, like a sensible person. You can understand that. He hadn't tried to pull away from 'Dart bodily, though, before the brawl."

Alrathe put hand to chin and rubbed. "Ulrad didn't mention the name of the other adventurer, the one with bluemetal work to sell? Or do you remember?"

"No. Ulrad had forgotten that adventurer's name, and he gave a short little description that could fit any number of people: tall, broad shoulders, nothing else."

"Mmm."

"Cousin Judge," said the storycrafter, "I don't know whether it will soften my guilt or sharpen it, but I hadn't drunk any wine yet. I hadn't drunk anything more volatile

all afternoon than a cup of mild cider Torin transformed out
of water for me in the Scholars' Tent."

"Perhaps if you had had a little wine in you, this would
not have happened," Alrathe remarked kindly. "Though the
stuff brittles some tempers, it dulls others. Not that I would
recommend drunkenness as a corrective for ready anger,
but this time when you go to Hilshar for salve ask her to
mix you a strong brandy posset as well."

"Not too strong." Dilys drank the last of her tea. "I have
to mount the platform in a few hours, and I'd better have
my steadiest brain and tongue. I'll want all I can earn this
fair, if I have to pay Kasdan the full twenty pebbles."

Alrathe inquired, "Do you know where Valdart went to
wait?"

The storycrafter nodded. "Laderan's tent. I went to
Mother Vathilda's, 'Dart went to Laderan's. Saying he'd
prefer skyreaders' company to that of magic-mongers."

"Send the adventurer to me when you leave," the judge
instructed her in friendly tones, by way of dismissal.

Alrathe would have expected the adventurer to choose
cordial, but Valdart wished none of a beverage he called
"neither stinging nor sober—just teasing like a silly child,"
and drank savoury herbwater instead.

Valdart's account of his conversation with merchant
Ulrad matched the storycrafter's well enough, allowing for
quirks of individual memory. Valdart seemed to accept
Ulrad's tale of a second pendant in good faith, and Alrathe
decided not to probe him at this time and risk raising suspicions where none might exist.

"But by Kasdan's testimony, his tent was not crowded
an hour ago," the judge pointed out. "You should have had
room to walk without treading on the Senior Storycrafter."

"She was sitting beside the straight footpath to the door.
I took that way going in. Why shouldn't I take it going
out?"

"Nevertheless, again according to the meal-merchant,

she was sitting squarely on her cushion, with her legs tucked in, not sprawling over the bare floormat."

"Brother Kasdan wasn't at any angle to see details. Not from what I noticed of where he was."

"Then she was sprawled to invite your kick?"

"I didn't say that," the adventurer grumbled. "But . . ."

"But you have no especial personal affection for the Senior Storycrafter?"

"I don't have any special dislike for her, either," said Valdart. "But Dil can be a directing, bothersome creature. The other night she even tried to direct me how to play Torinel's friend—me who was childhooding with him years before she knew either of us. Wanted me to go to Tor's tent and comfort him about his brother, talk him out of turning wizard himself in Talmar's place. Seems she didn't feel quite equal to comforting him herself, for all she thinks she knows his mind better than I do."

"Perhaps you should have considered her advice more carefully last night," said the judge, pondering how Valdart had three-syllabled his old friend's name in one sentence and single-syllabled it in the next. For a moment, the adventurer must have forgotten his grievances concerning Sharys and the missing pendant, in a kind of possessive friendship that disliked anyone else seeming to replace an old childhood comrade. "Your very manner of denying personal dislike for Dilys, however," Alrathe continued, "suggests that you do in fact feel it."

"How's that?" Valdart stood so quickly that hot tea splashed from his cup to his hand. He uttered a wordless exclamation and sat again. "Caught in a blamed leaky boat! You're the judge, Cousin. Is it fair judgment to make denials mean the same thing as confessions?"

"It is fair judgment to distinguish sincerity from lies, even unwitting lies. Although Dilys blocked your way and began that particular round of harsh words which resulted in damage to the meal-merchant's property, it appears she would probably have retained self-control and let you pass without conversation had you not trodden on her leg."

"Well, we'll never know, will we? Besides, it was accidental."

"So, in a sense, was the overturned brazier and resulting damage."

"I suppose that means you'll make me pay for it."

"I will give final judgment tomorrow morning. But in all likelihood I'll find it fair that you pay one third."

Valdart muttered some adventurers' expression of displeasure and went on, "I'm planning to marry this winter, Cousin Judge! I'll need all the moneygems I can save."

"Unexpected rockslides of expenses fall across everyone's path from time to time," Alrathe remarked.

"Another wise saw from some poet?"

"Aralyson, though she did not limit the observation to expense. And I must judge according to how actions and circumstances divide responsibility for damage, not according to how well or ill those responsible can afford to pay. Of course, you may attempt persuading Kasdan to cancel your share of the payment. Or you may have to forgo buying another expensive marriage token and trust that your chosen cares sincerely enough to accept a cheap one. Matings based on the simple expense of the marriage toy are often said not to be among the happiest."

Valdart set down his half-drunk cup of herbwater and stood again. "With respect, Cousin Judge, how much can you know about marrying?"

"Only wise saws gathered from poets," Alrathe replied, unoffended. "I will see you tomorrow morning in Kasdan's meal tent to pronounce my final judgment in this matter. Meanwhile, you are forewarned."

"Aye. And if you happen to earn your fee in that little complaint I brought you, and get me back my orangestone piece, I hope you won't mind sending for me before morning."

"If I do not recover your pendant, you need pay me nothing."

Valdart caught up the doorcurtain and left. As Alrathe

rose to refill the small kettle, Kara came in with Ulrad.

The judge nodded to them. "You'll have passed Valdart on his way from my tent."

"Back toward the meal-merchant's," Kara replied. "Doubting you need me any longer tonight, Cousin, I think I may buy some refreshment there myself now. Shall I knot the doorcords?"

Alrathe nodded again. "Aye, tie them for us, Cousin, and thanks for your help."

She smiled and ducked outside. The curtain swayed and bumped for a few moments as she tied the cords. Ulrad shifted his weight from one foot to the other and back.

"Tea or cordial?" Alrathe asked him.

"Oh, cordial, cordial. Unless it's made from pears. I never refuse cordial, uh, Cousin Alrathe. Unless it's pear cordial."

"This is made from cherries." Alrathe wiped the glass Kara had used, filled it again and handed it to Ulrad. Only a mouthful of cold tea remained in the judge's cup now, but that was enough to justify turning cup between fingers while waiting until fresh water boiled.

Ulrad took a triple sip of cordial, coughed, and wiped his mouth on a finely woven handycloth. "Well," he said. "I, uh, really can't remember myself at fault in this business, Cousin, but if—"

Alrathe waved one hand. "Valdart's and the story-crafter's accounts agree well enough. You were not to blame. Indeed, had you tried more strenuously to pull away, the damage might have been worse."

Ulrad relaxed visibly. "Then you don't want to hear my account?"

"I would have wished to hear it in full had you indicated you were going to assign yourself more blame than the others had given you, but where all others concerned absolve some person, that person rarely self-accuses."

Ulrad relaxed another degree. "Then this interview is just for appearances, eh? Balance. I can drink this tasty cordial and go about my business. Hard on merchants to

keep us from our business when we weren't even at fault in
some matter."

"When I arranged to interview you as well as the others,
I could not know they would absolve you."

Ulrad drank the rest of his cordial and patted his lips
with the handycloth. "You won't want me tomorrow morning in the mealseller's pavilion, either, then. When you tell
the others your judgment."

"I will want you. For balance. You'll want breakfast, no
doubt, and it should not require too much of your time
before that meal."

"Oh. Yes, yes, of course. For balance." Ulrad put down
the empty glass and shifted as if preparing to get to his
feet.

"Nevertheless," Alrathe said carefully, "though I cannot
in fairness direct you to pay any share of the expenses, I
am curious about your reluctance to sell Valdart this second
bluemetal pendant."

Ulrad picked up his glass again and looked at the few
drops sliding slowly down into the bottom. "I just bought
that piece in this neighborhood, Cousin-Judge Alrathe. We
can't sell things again in the same neighborhood where we
buy 'em. Not us traveling merchants. No profit in that. I
was trying to explain all that sort of thing to you just this
morning when you asked me about it, if you remember?"

"Valdart said he offered to pay you whatever you would
ask for it in another neighborhood. That seems fair, and no
loss to your profit."

Ulrad shrugged.

"Perhaps the adventurer remembers voicing an offer that
in fact passed only through his brain without escaping in
words to reach your ears?"

"No . . . no, he did make the offer. Aye, I remember it
now. But it'd be bad practice, Cousin. Very bad example,
unsound habit to start." Ulrad shook his head.

"The circumstances are unusual. Surely you could make
one exception to your usual practice without beginning a
new habit."

"No!" Another headshake. "See this, Cousin Judge. Can you just scatter exceptions into your judgework wherever you want 'em?"

Alrathe avoided a discussion of the balance between absolute justice and individual circumstances. Good judges spent their entire lives climbing after that ideal balance, but Ulrad did not seem the kind of layperson with whom to speak of it. "Having such a toy is very important to the adventurer this season. In his mind, it seems closely tied to his whole future, whether he will marry and settle, or continue wandering." Or marry and continue wandering, the judge added mentally.

"I can't help that," said Ulrad. "He should've kept closer watch on his own pendant last night."

"I do not remember seeing his pendant before its disappearance. It begins to appear I am the only person at this Amberleaf fair not to have seen him show it off. But I understand yours is its identical twin. If I could—"

"Not identical. No, not so very much alike, not at all."

"Oh? I understood you yourself made the claim. As similar as two walnuts?"

"Ah, that." Ulrad shrugged. "Mealshop jabber, Cousin. Mealshop jabber. Now I think of it, Valdart's was much finer crafted. Aye, mine'd look shoddy beside it. So if he does get it back, Cousin, I'm still eager to buy his."

"I'd meant to ask a chance to examine yours," said Alrathe, "so as to learn better what I am looking for. But since the two pieces are not so similar after all, I can spend my time more usefully otherwhere."

"Aye, Cousin, aye. I can go about my business now?"

"One more thing. Dilys and Valdart testify that part of her reason for blocking your way was that you have not yet paid the toymaker for what you took yesterday from his showledge."

"Oh. Ah, yes. Well, I couldn't find him this morning, and he's been busy in the Scholars' Pavilion all afternoon. I'd...uh...leave the moneygems with you or Cousin Dilys, if you could tell me the total."

"The toymaker was in his tent for most of this morning. When did you try to find him?"

"Ah." Another shrug. "Well, Cousin Judge, you understand. Doorcords, busy inside, don't interrupt, your own neighborhood manners. I meant I couldn't find him outside and unoccupied."

Judge gazed steadily at merchant. "Only Torin can tell you the total. But no tradecrafter would be wise to acquire a reputation for slippery dealings in our neighborhood, Cousin Ulrad, however accidental and undeserved that reputation may be. I advise you to settle with the toymaker before you come to Kasdan's meal tent tomorrow, even if you must wait in the Scholars' Pavilion until he finishes his showcrafting there this evening."

"Yes. Yes, of course. Good notion, Cousin Judge. Thanks. Shouldn't be too much longer." Ulrad drank the last few drops of collected cordial and set down the glass. "I can go now? Make sure to catch him."

Alrathe nodded. "I have nothing more to ask you, Cousin Merchant. Prosper in your trade and in your blamelessness."

"And you, Cousin. Prosper." Ulrad bowed, clumsily but eagerly, and departed.

Watching the curtain swing back into place, Alrathe sighed and hoped the merchant had not been overly alarmed. That last piece of questioning had been the afternoon's most delicate interview, and the judge was far from self-content.

At least the meal tent brawl had, in itself, been fairly easy to judge. And it might have provided further pieces of the orangestone puzzle. "If I can only fit together the business of High Wizard Talmar and his wandering globe . . ." the judge murmured, looking again at the lists of transformed banquet foods.

Alrathe's fingertip came down on the line "dewmelons." Yesterday's had been transformed from cabbages, as testified both by the conjurer's list and Alrathe's own memory of seeing transformations unknit on the table. According to

Torin's list, the dewmelons for Talmar's First Name-Lengthening dinner had probably been made from pumpkins, but it was long ago and that was one of several transformations the toymaker remained unsure about.

Alrathe stood and removed the steaming kettle from the brazier. Another visit to the sick wizard's tent might not be misplaced this evening.

Twelve

THE TOYMAKER HOPED Vathilda would not decide to continue their magic show throughout supper hour. Such practices could be profitable at larger fairs, where customary mealtimes caused comparatively little pause in other trade, due to the numbers of people who ate at unusual hours or bypassed some meals altogether. But this last Amberleaf Fair of the season was too small.

The old sorceress obviously recognized this. When the clouded sky began darkening early, she announced that, like the storytellers, the magickers would tie their door-strings for supper and start the evening's entertainment an hour after full dark, at which time Torin would climb the platform.

Inside the alcove for private shows, Torin heard her, saw anticipation on his last buyer's face, and felt—instead of relief—a shiver. He sat alone in the alcove until by the fading sounds, the last members of the audience had gone. When he came out, only Vathilda remained in the outer tent, the other students having presumably gone with the showbuyers.

"I wish you had not announced I would begin tonight's platform show," the toymaker said with careful calm.

"You agreed to that plan at midday."

"I felt less tired at midday." Or perhaps, more guilty. "And I didn't expect so many feats to go wrong for me in the alcove this afternoon."

"They'll buy to see your mistakes as readily as your successes, Brother Crafter."

"I know. . . . Well, half an hour, then. Seven tricks."

"An hour, and repeat your seven. Half an hour's hardly time enough to fetch 'em in."

"Well, then. At least I can give my brother this evening if I can't promise him the rest of my life."

"You've made your final choice, eh?"

"I made it when I was fifteen years old." The toymaker shrugged. "I find it hasn't changed."

"If all of us rethought our choice after every long show afternoon," said Vathilda, "precious few would stay with the study, and those few the frivolous ones, the applause-crafters. Displays are the least of magic-mongering."

"I know."

"But not the least dangerous, for some."

"That I'm not sure of."

"Aye," said Vathilda, with another shrewd glance, "it's glory-chokers who run most risks on that platform, and I doubt you're one to fall under that rockslide. But if your brother's dying, do him one kindness and don't tell him you're fixed on staying crafter."

"Not unless he sews me into a pocket." Torin was not among those few strict folk who believed painful truths pleased Cel more than kindly falsehoods, but somehow he did not want to send Talmar to Thyrna the Harvest Spirit with this particular lie. Perhaps he feared that if he uttered any such statement, Vathilda would find some way, after all, of transforming it into truth? "But hope seemed better this afternoon that he's not dying."

He might be dead or fully recovered; close as Talmar's tent was, they had received no news to interrupt their show.

Vathilda shrugged and led the way from the Scholars' Pavilion. When Torin was outside with her, she dropped behind to stiffen the doorcurtain. He walked on to the high wizard's tent.

Talmar's curtain hung stiff, but suppled at his brother's touch. Talmar was asleep, and—unexpectedly—Dilys was here. She sat to one side, out of the way, a steaming cup in her hands, and when she caught Torin's glance she nodded back toward the sick man, whose sleep seemed much easier now. Sharys knelt beside him, her head and forearms on the bed near his chest. At first it looked like despair, but Torin saw she had fallen asleep, too. Talmar's breathing sounded nearly normal except for a thin whine somewhere high in his nose. The last of the swelling had gone down, and only a few speckles of rash remained on his face. In health and repose, a handsome face, longer and thinner than his brother's, with a clifflike rather than a gentle nose, but a paler complexion since the high wizard spent little time outdoors. Torin had sometimes carved statues of Vikal, Spirit of the North Wind and Winter, with Talmar for a remembered model.

"Aye, out of danger, I think," Hilshar murmured near Torin. He looked around and saw she had come up from behind, bringing a bottle of cordial. She must have been preparing it when he came in. "We found Sharys asleep like that," the magician added, "and didn't want to wake her just yet."

Torin looked again at Talmar and Sharys. For a moment he wondered . . . yet her arm was browner than Talmar's cheek. Her summer-gathered sunbronze had not faded very much.

Vathilda came in with a billow of draft. "Tender scene," Torin heard her mutter to Hilshar. Then the old sorceress touched his shoulder. "I just met that traveling merchant, Brother Crafter. Outside our Scholars' Tent. Said he was looking to pay you what he owes. I told him to come back for our evening display."

Dilys half choked on a wry chuckle. "Scurrying ants

and skelter-trails! Maybe you can still catch him, Torinel."

Torin returned to the door and looked out. He could not see either of the far-traveling merchants who still owed him for toys taken yesterday, and he did not relish the idea of a tag-chase along muddy footpaths. Business was not quite that important, especially here.

When he turned back into the tent, Vathilda was shaking her granddaughter's shoulder. Sharys woke and lifted her head. Talmar opened his eyes at the same moment.

"Sleep-headed healers soothe only themselves," said Vathilda. "Go catch some proper rest, sapling. Your mother and I can watch for a few hours."

Sharys protested a little. "I didn't. I didn't drowse until . . ." Her hand moved toward Talmar's chest. His hand came up to cover hers.

Talmar's glance stirred through the tent and he smiled, though keeping his lips slightly parted as if for easier breathing. "All right, all right, Sharilysin." His voice was still a little ragged, but his words were steady. "It seems I've gathered four more nurses. Go and rest."

She looked at his face. He closed his eyes, and Torin thought the veins bulged in his high forehead . . . not much. If he was indeed adding a mind-message, her obvious receptivity, coupled with their physical nearness, meant it cost him little strain. Perhaps she closed her eyes also, but her back was to the toymaker. After a moment she nodded, stood, and turned to go.

Dilys sighed and sipped from her cup.

"Well?" said Vathilda. "Contented with her nursing, are you, Son Talmar?"

"Well contented, Daughter Vathilda."

Sharys paused and glanced back, then reached for the doorcurtain. It looked almost as if she were gesturing it to one side without touching it. By coincidence—it must be —Judge Alrathe was just coming in.

"I think probably you should stay a few moments longer, Cousin Sharys," said the judge. "Ah! Cousin Talmar, you look happily near-recovered."

"And feel so." Lifting handycloth to mouth, the wizard coughed as if to clear his throat and went on, marginally less hoarse, "I'll give the closing display tomorrow evening, as planned."

Vathilda grunted. "Ah? Then best keep to simple tricks. No more showing off new fancies with your fool's globe."

"Mother Vathilda." The judge fingered a writing tablet. "With every respect for your skills as healer, I remarked yesterday that this resembled sensitivity."

Vathilda looked at Alrathe, curled her left hand against her right and snapped all four finger-knuckles simultaneously. "How often have you seen glory-choking, Child Judge?"

"Not often. Buying and receiving judgments is not an activity that fosters pride. I have seen anger-choking, however, and two of my birth cousins have suffered from curious sensitivities. I assume that boasting sickness more nearly resembles anger-choking than sensitivity."

Hilshar crossed to the bed, sat down and began rubbing Talmar's forehead with a damp cloth. "We should consider every possibility, Mother."

"Aye, maybe."

"Or are you too proud, Sister Vathilda?" said Talmar.

The sorceress coughed and folded her arms. "So, Cousin Judge. Rather than be accused of boasting myself, I'll hear your notion."

Alrathe opened the tablet. "My cousin Therian's sensitivity is especially curious. Cherries and peaches she can eat alone with no trouble, provided she allows at least a day between. But if she eats both at the same meal, she chokes and swells much as Cousin Talmar did yesterday, though not so desperately. Since those two fruits are often served together, we were able to identify her sensitivity in time to plan a safe feast for her First Name-Lengthening."

"Convenient," said Vathilda. "Aye, I've heard of these double sensitivities. Rarely."

"Now, suppose one of the mischievous foods were transformed from the other? And that it was not the usual base food, but an infrequently used substitute."

"It might happen seldom and slip unrecognized for years," said Talmar. "As mine did."

Vathilda looked at him. "You guessed all this in your sick dreams, Son? Or did our healer-judge consult you before me?"

"You were busy all day with the show, Grandmother," said Sharys. "And we had to make up the food lists for Cousin Alrathe."

"Inconveniently," said Talmar, "I took no part in preparing my First Name-Lengthening dinner. We have only my brother's memory for that." He looked at Torin and Torin looked away, feeling, however irrationally, that he had been accused and somehow deserved it.

"We must assume the mischievous combination is among those Torin never knew or has not remembered," said the judge. "But what poet has advised us to keep careful memory storage of dinners, even First Name-Lengthening dinners, that we ate twenty years ago? Poets who mention it at all tend to praise forgetfulness in such cases. Cousin Hilshar, did you use any unusual base liquid for the wines?"

She shook her head. "Plain water transforms into anything else drinkable. I did mingle some milk with it for the cordials."

"I fell sick before drinking any cordial," said Talmar.

"No more did I make any inventive changes," said Vathilda. "I've learned better than to experiment when there's no need."

Alrathe consulted the writing tablet. "Then, assuming a lapse in Torin's memory, I suspect either citrons made from potatoes or dewmelons from cabbages."

"The melons!" said Talmar. "I've made citrons for myself from potatoes."

"And whatever else," said Torin. "He's relished citrons since growing his teeth. But yes! We might have transformed our dewmelons from cabbages for his dinner if pumpkins were scarce that year."

"Aye," said Vathilda. "Neat and tidy, Cousin Judge, and how will we prove it, eh?"

"Transform another one," said the high wizard. "Another cabbage into dewmelon. I'll eat it tomorrow night. After my display of magic."

"Talmariak!" exclaimed Sharys, starting back to him.

"Not the safest kind of test, Uncle Talmar," Dilys was remarking.

"Yes. A rugged harvesting. I know what I'll risk. More clearly than any of you." Talmar paused, looking around at all of them and coughing deliberately into his cloth. "I will dazzle this fair tomorrow evening. Five towns will envy everyone who came here and saw my new techniques first. Afterwards, I'll eat the transformation. If I survive my display and choke on the cabbage-melon, we'll know."

"And either you'll meet Thyrna in earnest this time, or keep us here three days after the fair nursing you again," said Vathilda.

"Talmarak." Torin swallowed. His brother had not questioned him into any tangible pocket, yet it felt that way. He avoided looking at Vathilda. "Whatever happens, Talmariak, whatever you do or choose against, I'll remain a toycrafter. Don't walk your knife-edge path hoping otherwise."

Talmar breathed a deep sigh that ended in something like another half-cough. "Will you, then? Still the fool, ever—always our family fool, older brother? Well, I won't eat much. Only enough to prove sensitivity."

"Fools think every path's a knife-edge but their own," said Vathilda. "I'd avoid glory-climbing and cabbage-dewmelons both, Son Talmar, but if you're determined on risking your magic show, is that any reason to risk the melon too? Glory-choke on your fine display, and I'll stay to nurse you again. Choke on your melon afterward, and I'll take my family home and leave whoever chooses to nurse you."

Staring at her grandmother, Sharys slipped her hand into Talmar's. "You don't even like dewmelons so very much,

do you, Uncle Talmariak? And I'd have to make it. Maybe
it was something in my magic that made the combination
mischievous."

After a moment he smiled, seemed to squeeze her hand
and then shake it away. "When I survive my magic display,
Sister Vathilda, agree this must have been sensitivity and
stop trying to humble me. But if I do glory-choke on my
own achievements tomorrow, leave me to die. Don't nurse
me again."

"And you won't try eating cabbage-melons?" said
Sharys.

Talmar smiled at her and shook his head.

"Aye, well," said the sorceress. "A foolish bargain, but
I'll agree to it. Now come back to our own tent, Sharys
sapling, and rest for an hour. You'll help me with the evening show and we'll leave your mother to nurse our stubborn fool of a wizard. Toymaker, you're still magicker with
us until midnight, however you choose the rest of your
life."

"I'll be ready an hour after full dark." Torin watched
Vathilda take her granddaughter's arm and draw her from
the tent. He sighed, brushed his fingers over his hair, and
looked at Dilys.

She looked down into her cup. "I've almost finished.
Thank you for the posset, Mother Hilshar." She swallowed
a last mouthful, set the cup down, and glanced back at
Torin. "I've finished."

"But I have not," said Judge Alrathe. "Not quite. I have
still something to ask you, Cousin Talmar."

"Ah?" Talmar's brow wrinkled a little. "Concerning
some judgment, Cousin? I think I'm strong enough to lie
here nurseless awhile."

Dilys stood, and Hilshar put down her damp cloth.

But Alrathe answered them with a headshake. "I doubt
any judgment is involved. Only the answer to a troublesome puzzle. High Wizard, last night you yourself arranged for someone to take your globe to your brother's
tent."

Talmar looked from Alrathe to Torin and shrugged. "That puzzled you? Last night I thought I saw the Harvest Spirit clear. One last message for my brother. Brother Torin, I fancied you'd see its meaning as clearly as I saw Thyrna with her harvest hook."

This time the toymaker shrugged. "I didn't, Talmar. Not entirely. I thought perhaps I'd walked asleep, taken it in my dreams. I thought . . ." He let his voice trail off. It was his self-doubts about taking Talmar's globe unconsciously that had planted his self-doubts about taking Valdart's orangestone in the same way, but he found little reason to speak of that here.

"If my thoughts muddled last night," said Talmar, "I had some excuse."

"I also believe I could name your messenger," said Alrathe.

"Perhaps," the wizard replied indifferently. "That person made secrecy a condition, and I'll respect my promise."

"I guessed as much," said the judge. "That was why you scrambled the images for the time your messenger must have been with you receiving your instructions."

"Scrambling the images was simple. Thinking reason gave me more difficulty last night. But I did realize that having muddled a few moments, I had only to let my globe continue reviewing and it would not absorb my messenger's reflection during the rest of our talk."

Hilshar looked at Alrathe. "But we were with him together, never fewer than two or three of us, all afternoon until evening, and then we all left him alone for Thyrna."

"Mind-messages," replied the judge.

"But he was too weak to send mind-messages any distance." Hilshar picked up the damp cloth again, turning it absently in her hands. "So it had to be one of us who were with him there."

"Exactly," said the judge. "In the afternoon, Cousin Talmar, you sent a mind-message to one of us in the tent with you, telling that person to come find you in your own tent when you were alone for the night."

"Use the name, if you think you know it." The high
wizard coughed a little. "I won't say whether you're right
or wrong. But it might be more convenient for you."

Some of Torin's newly discarded fear revived. "You sent
me at least one mind-message."

"And you shut your mind to me. Mind-messages don't
slip in beneath the listener's awareness, Brother. And no
one can mind-message another into doing something dis-
tasteful. I tried to break that simple principle often enough
with you when we were saplings. Before you left us."

"That may explain some of my childhood nightmares,"
Torin remarked. "But you'll assure us it wasn't me?"

"It was not you, Brother," Talmar said wearily. "If you
don't remember the principle in question, maybe you
wouldn't make a good magic-monger, after all. I don't try
to play with it any longer. Not since I turned responsible
magician."

"Did you give your messager a counter-charm to neu-
tralize the one in Torin's doorcords?" asked the judge.

"No." Talmar glanced at the storyteller. "You'll assume
that means it was a fellow-magicker."

"No," replied the judge. "But if it was a layperson, that
person must have realized, or you must have explained,
that our charms keep out only those who plan mischief.
Bringing something into a tent is hardly a deed any charm
would recognize as theft or mischief, no matter how much
the puzzle might afterwards trouble the recipient."

"Clever, Cousin Judge." Talmar turned to Dilys. "Now
may we ask you not to put it into your tales, Sister Storycrafter?"

"If I told stories about that sort of thing, I'd have put in
such a trick long ago."

"Well." Talmar coughed—it seemed involuntary this
time, though still undesperate—lay back and motioned for
Hilshar to dab his forehead. "Yes. I saw my messenger in
the afternoon and sent a mind-message. Although at that
moment my plans were no more than half glimpsed. The

person accepted my message, came to my tent later, agreed to do my errand in return for secrecy. And payment in moneygems. Most of my last remaining gems. I thought I'd have no further use for them, and hoped my other property would recompense my nurses. I did not need to give my messenger a counter-charm. I will not say whether because it was a fellow magicker or because I had to explain the trick of not intending mischief. I doubt I could have crafted a counter-charm last night. It's not a commonly practiced skill. I suppose I've only confirmed what you guessed, Cousin Judge."

"Clarified it," said Alrathe. "And, I think, relieved your brother of a greater mental burden than you might suspect. When will you take your globe back, Cousin Wizard?"

"Tomorrow morning," Hilshar answered for Talmar.

Talmar turned his head to look at her and shrugged slightly. "Aye. Tomorrow morning. To prevent any new sleep-robbing excitement in the high wizard's lungs tonight."

Outside Talmar's tent the three paused. Drizzle still fell, but all wore drycharms, and the toymaker and storyteller seemed uncertain whether to separate or walk together. Alrathe turned away first. The judge's crimson tent was only a few steps from Talmar's, in the opposite direction to the main fairground.

"Cousin Judge," Torin said softly, "Talmar's messenger was also the one who took Valdart's pendant?"

"Most probably, I think. It seems overmuch coincidence that different individuals should stumble into the trick on the same night."

"And it wasn't me!"

"I think," said Dilys, "only two people ever seriously suspected our toymaker: Valdart, and Torinel himself."

They did not ask who the judge believed responsible. Such revelations were left to judges' discretion, often kept strictly private between judge, complainant, and culprit. "Thank you, Cousin Alrathe," said Torin. Then, taking the

storyteller's hand, "We have time for two of Kasdan's suppers before our evening's work."

"I'm not sure I want to go back to Kasdan's pavilion.
Not until tomorrow morning, at least. That's where I
caught this limp a few hours ago, Torinel. Wine-brawling
for the sake of your business."

"The good mealcrafter will have his judgment tomorrow
morning," said Alrathe, before Torin could comment.
"And his moneygems as soon after that as you can pay
them."

"I intend to bring a full pouch along to the judgment,"
said Dilys.

"'Prudence is the stem of mannerliness,'" Alrathe
quoted one of the anonymous poets. "Meanwhile, Cousin,
if you can swim through Kasdan's supper crowd, you
might find it easier to sit above your story audience afterward."

She sighed. "And this began as such a proud little fair
for me."

"I have to climb the Scholars' Tent platform and muddle
magic feats for the first hour this evening," said Torin.
"Mother Vathilda's schedule. Show me how to meet
chuckles calmly, Dilysin."

She joined hands with him. "Well, Brother Crafter, let's
go buy our meal, then. You can reassure Kasdan you'll
hold me back if another brawl starts to bud out, and when
folk see us supping together, it may help stir up even more
interested audiences for both our pavilions tonight."

Judge Alrathe did not go to the mealseller's tent, but
supped alone that night, pondering small details.

Thirteen

KASDAN'S MEAL TENT was crowded, but Torin and Dilys found a corner just being vacated. Kasdan glanced at them but made no audible comment.

Halfway across the tent, Ulrad sat alone, sipping some beverage. Beyond him, on the far side, Valdart and Kara were sharing a meal. Torin caught sight of them, but decided against threading his way amongst the other meal-buyers to them. Perhaps he was shy of approaching Kara for his money while Valdart looked on. He glimpsed more clearly what he and the judge had done in urging Dilys to return and buy supper from Kasdan; if her guilt was actual and Torin's existed only in Valdart's suspicion, still Kasdan was a mere acquaintance to her and Valdartak an old friend to the toymaker. No doubt these factors balanced.

"Maybe you could tell the adventurer that Judge Alrathe considers you innocent of taking his glittergem," Dilys suggested.

Torin shook his head and sat facing her, admiring her apparent calm. Both sat cross-legged, and his right knee touched her left. In the cramped conditions of the meal tent, neither tried to shift away and break contact.

Kasdan's daughter Danys came, asked their preferences, and exchanged short, commonplace pleasantries. When she had crafted her way back between the mealbuyers, Kara approached along the path she had followed. Torin was hardly aware of the merchant's coming until Dilys remarked on it.

Kara reached them, half knelt for easier conversation, and said, "How much is it I owe you, Brother Toycrafter?" She spoke as if no time had lapsed between the hour she chose her purchases and now, but Torin had to think before answering, to recall the totals he had reckoned from the storyteller's notes, and to be sure he was not confusing Kara's total with Ulrad's.

"You took the statuette of Ilfting and his three porcupines, the miniature Haven-house, four pinecone-section necklaces and one set of inlaid gamepieces?"

Kara nodded. "Also an assortment of smaller toys and tokens."

"Forty-three pebbles, one small stone and four large."

Kara counted them out, said she might return at fair's end and examine his remaining stock, inquired when Dilys would climb the storytellers' platform this evening, wished them a comfortable night, and returned to Valdart. A moment after she had left the path clear, Ulrad came trundling along to ask the toymaker what he owed.

"Fifty-six pebbles?" he repeated on hearing it. "You're sure?"

"If you'd rather find me tomorrow and check through the list . . ." Torin felt overtired to attempt comparison by memory.

Ulrad glanced around and cleared his throat. "No—no, I'm sure you're right. You do know your own business, eh? Aye, a shrewd seller. Fifty-six pebbles, two small stones and three large, it was?" He counted them onto the floormat at a careful distance from Kara's pile, heaved himself to his feet, wished them well almost as if it was an

afterthought, and worked his way back to his place in time
to take his mealplate from Kasdan, who had just brought it.

Some buyers along the path had begun to look slightly
annoyed at the traffic, but now that it seemed to be over
except for the mealsellers' movements, they settled again
to their food. Torin scooped most of Kara's and Ulrad's
payments into his moneypouch. The gems that would not
fit he pocketed loose. Had such an amount of money come
to him at another time, he thought, the unusual weight in
pouch and pockets would have given him a special thrill;
but somehow tonight it seemed another simple, necessary
detail of everyday business.

"I think Kara nudged Ulrad on her way to us and again
on her way back," said Dilys, who faced the main part of
the tent.

"Can you see Valdartak's expression?"

"No."

Vathilda did keep the Scholars' Pavilion doorcurtains
open until midnight. Torin spent only the first hour showing off his clumsinesses on the platform before returning to
the alcove, but he still had two buyers waiting for private
demonstrations, Boken the furniture crafter and Kara's adventurer Vittor, after the last members of the general audience departed. The rain had stopped.

Tired though he was, he went to Dilysin's tent rather
than his own, half hoping it would be dark and her doorcords knotted. It was dark, but the cords hung loose. Perhaps she had fallen asleep forgetting to tie them. If so, he
would do it for her. He pulled her curtain back a little and
called in very softly, "Dilysin?"

"Torinel. Come in."

The only light inside came from her brazier. She sat on
the other side of its glow, a huddled shape dark against the
slightly less dark cloth walls, which were a little illumined
from without, the neighboring tent's lantern casting
shadow patterns for her background. The scholars' section
of any fairground was left dark, largely for skyreaders'

convenience, but in the layfolks' sections a thick candle or
small lantern with large oil reservoir usually burned all
night in front of every fourth or fifth tent, giving enough
light for late walkers to find their way, but not enough to
hinder sleep.

Torin went in. Dilys stood, stretched her legs, and lifted
kettle to brazier. "Drink a cup of herbwater with me. Or
would you rather drink cordial?" Her voice sounded marginally hoarse.

"Herbwater and cordial together?" he suggested.

"Good. Sweetblend and plum."

They sat side by side on her bed while waiting for the
water to boil.

"I hope your storytelling went better than my magic-
mongering."

"It went very well. I was surprised." She coughed. "I
don't think it's another sensitivity, like Talmar's. I think
it's a chilled throat. I should have worn my drycharm all
along, and I put too much strain on my throatcharm today.
Convenient that the last-night magic show closes the Storytellers' Pavilion by evening. And I may not do my afternoon session tomorrow. I won't really need to. With the
money I gathered tonight, I'll be able to pay Kasdan's
damages without digging into my fund for this winter." She
coughed again and rewrapped her scarf around her neck.
"Your turn, Torinel. Talk, or I'll keep on, and my throat
doesn't want to."

He had trouble deciding what to say. "A good crowd
came to watch me bumble the platform show. Then I think
most of them went to hear your tales."

"Mine and Valdart's. I followed him this evening."

"And then they must have come back for private shows
in my alcove. I'm afraid your other tellers might have been
cheated of their audience."

"We kept the fairgoers bouncing tonight, didn't we? We
could really have split them if I'd scheduled Valdart or
myself first, at the same time you were platforming. I'm
glad I made the fair's whole schedule the first day." She

sighed. "Torinel, I don't like gathering audiences because of gossip. It makes nice profits, but I don't like it."

"I know. It's the difference between selling well-made toys and selling magic feats done clumsily."

"Let's never become hubs for gossip again. No matter how good it is for trade."

"A beautiful plan."

"Except it was hardly your fault this fair. But it was mine. I made a gossip-hub of myself."

Rain started falling once more, or the kettle prepared to boil, or both.

"Gossip-hubs," said Torin. "If it's an accurate image. The hub stays in the middle, comparatively quiet. The wheel's rim collects the dust and mud."

"The hub gets a few splatters now and then. How many people think wheels are worth charms against dirt?" She rose to put spoonfuls of sweetblend tea and dollops of plum cordial into the cups. "Besides, the hub's not so quiet. It whirls around faster than the rim. The larger the wheel, the faster spins the hub. I think."

"Did we get all this image from one of the poets?"

"Probably." She poured boiling water, set the kettle down beneath the brazier, handed Torin his cup and sat again, cradling hers between her fingertips. "Torinel, how much have you read in ancient books?"

"Very little. Even when I was still a student, so many old writings seemed incomprehensible."

"So many of them are."

"Of course, I was very young."

"It's not only a person's age that makes them incomprehensible. In fact, sometimes I think I understood more of them when I was a sapling than I do now. False comprehension, maybe." She shook her head.

"And then, magic-mongers and skyreaders concentrate on their own narrow paths through the archives. Judges and storycrafters read as wide a horizon as they can. You story-crafters are almost students, aren't you?"

"Not all storycrafters mine old archives. So much an-

cient material is too ugly to be useful. Assuming it means
more or less what it seems to mean. Gossip, for instance.
In ancient times, there seemed to be a lot more conscious
mischief in it, a lot less neighborly concern for the gossip-
hubs. We're a hub for curiosity and concern at this fair, and
we don't enjoy it, but our own shame hurts us more than
our neighbors' talk—I mean my shame, you don't have
any cause to be ashamed. But it'll fade, and meanwhile
almost everyone is still polite to us. In the old times, as
nearly as I can understand, gossip could destroy people's
whole lives—actually, like rockslides or disease—and
sometimes the folk who spread gossip seemed to plan such
results. I think that wheel image must come from one of
the earliest poets."

"I wonder if we've really climbed so high. I'm thinking
of Brother Elvar the music-crafter." Torin was also thinking of Valdart, whom he had always considered so close a
friend.

"Oh, Elvar. We find people like Elvar unpleasant, but
. . . Well, you may be right. What about me, wine-brawling
when I hadn't even drunk any wine? And yet. . ." She
flicked her memory through things she had read in the oldest writings, and found her own behavior, Elvar's, even
'Dart's gentle in comparison. "No, I'm not even going to
tell you some of the other ancient tales I've puzzled out."

"We still understand the gossip-wheel image, ancient or
not."

"But the ancients seemed to have other meanings for
dust and muck. As if they thought it was somehow insulting, immoral, not simply Cel's fertile earth made overwet
or smeared out of place." She decided to turn their conversation along another trail. "Did Merchant Kara come to
your pavilion?"

"Yes. For a private display. I don't think she was in my
earlier audience for the platform show."

"I heard she came to the Storytellers' Tent in time to
hear Kivin. She stayed to hear all my tales, then she must
have gone to your pavilion."

"That means she heard Valdart, doesn't it?"

"Yes."

"And she ate supper with him."

"Torinel," Dilys said softly, "I think perhaps we're gossiping now."

"I'm thinking of Sharilys."

"Well? Iris probably ate supper with Laderan, and you ate with me."

"Iris is Laderan's apprentice, and we're old friends."

"Kara's a traveling merchant who may need another adventurer or two, and Valdart's an adventurer."

Torin sipped his sweetblend and tried to remember his brief glimpse of Valdart's expression in the meal tent. "I was wondering what he might do if Sharys chooses elsewhere tomorrow, after all."

"Do you think she will choose elsewhere?"

"Yes. But not me."

They sat in silence for a while, drinking their hot herbwater and cordial, memories of the afternoon floating thick around them. "But suppose she does choose you?" Dilys said at last, not really expecting that she would.

"I don't know. I've made one decision at this fair. I'm not sure I'm ready to make another. Maybe it's not mine to make, not any longer. I did urge her . . . only yesterday? I'd be rude to change now, but unkind, maybe, to keep to it."

"I doubt that. You're very fond of each other. You've been good friends for years, as long as I've known you myself, Torinel, all the seasons she's been growing up. You'd climb together comfortably."

He was silent. He had not specified who would bear the weight of his unkindness.

"But suppose she doesn't choose you?" said Dilys.

"I seem to remember answering that this afternoon. When I offered you my toy." He tried to smile. "A fine piece of carving, to be refused twice in two days."

"Impulse?"

"No. Offering it to Sharys was a long, slow impulse. Offering it to you was sudden self-understanding."

She blinked. "Torinivel. I'd marry you tonight, without any token, if—Shh!"

He listened in confusion, hearing rain and small-creature noises.

"No," she whispered after a moment. "It's passed now."

"What?"

"I thought I heard a footstep. As if someone had stepped on an unexpected rock."

"Returning to the home tent, maybe. As I'll be doing in a little while."

"If it had been someone walking openly, why so silent most of the way? Why did I hear one or two steps and a little grunt instead of a whole trail of footfalls?" She shrugged. "Well, the rain, the mud. Maybe it was just another woods animal foraging for faircrumbs."

"Or that one statue of a donkey I couldn't animate when I wanted to on the platform, finally come alive and looking for me."

She chuckled, barely louder than an audible smile.

He finished his herbwater, put his cup down beside the kettle, and stood.

She stood with him. "But you said you weren't ready to make another life decision at this fair."

"Dilarysin. Some decisions make themselves."

They held each other.

"No," he said at last, "not with unpleasant business waiting in the morning."

"And if Sharilys should choose you, how polite a way would it be to make your refusal: 'I can't marry you after all, because I married someone else last night'?"

"Both of us overtired, one with a chilled throat, and animated statues trodding in the mud around the tent."

A soft, shared chuckle, a squeezing together that lasted no longer than a heartbeat, and they separated.

He looked around when he was outside her tent. As usual, she had put it up among those of the adventurers, where fairgrounds were comparatively quiet during daytime. He saw nothing of any person walking stealthily. On the way back to the crafters' section he passed a larger tent which he thought was either Kara's or Ulrad's.

On reaching his own tent, he checked carefully by globe-light, but found nothing gone and nothing added. He put his moneygems away and painted two new protective charms, one to knot with Talmar's into his doorcords and the other to tie around his traveling-chest. They were hasty, crude and temporary, due to his weariness and rustiness with this type of crafting, but they should work for tonight, and the extra safeguard, as well as the concentration required for charmcasting, helped him sleep better.

Fourteen

THE RAIN STOPPED in the night and the clouds dissolved by dawn. Early as Judge Alrathe arrived in Kasdan's meal tent, all involved parties except Valdart were waiting. Slightly more than the involved parties: Kara sat near Ulrad, sipping tea, as if they had come together.

Dilys sat a little apart, also sipping tea. Kasdan worked in his cooking-corner, ready to step forward when wanted. His daughter Danys worked with him. On the other side of the tent five people sat breakfasting. At first Alrathe thought they were completely uninvolved, but another glance showed them to be Camys the weaver, Boken the furniture crafter and his son, and Arlys and Tambur the metalsmiths, whom Kasdan would have consulted in fixing the exact cost of his damages.

"I thought it might save time to have them near at hand, in case of any questions," Kasdan explained, bowing to the judge. "Cousin, what if other early mealbuyers come before we're done here? I don't like losing business."

"You're the only mealseller at this Amberleaf Fair," said Dilys.

"Some folk might go back and dig into their own supplies sooner than stand outside my pavilion waiting to be let in."

Dilys bent her head and stared at the floormat. "Well, I don't object, so long as they sit on the far side, away from us."

"Nor I!" Ulrad said hastily.

"We'll hope Valdart arrives before other mealbuyers." Alrathe sat, forming a triangle with Dilys and the pair of merchants. "Cousin Kasdan, a cup of sweetblend?"

As the judge was speaking, Valdart brushed into the tent. "Morning wine for me. Your best. Double the spices and two-thirds the hot water."

"Greetings, adventurer," Dilys murmured.

Kara repeated the greeting more heartily, rising at the same time. "I assume you'll want me on the far side now," she added, looking around at them all. "Shall I take Danys with me by asking her to bring my food at once?"

"Damage to my property is damage to my daughter's," said the mealseller.

Kara nodded. "Fine. I'd hoped she'd have time to heat my breakfast thoroughly."

She crossed the tent and Valdart took the place she had left, sitting with one leg sprawling in front of him. The herbwater and morning wine were quickly mixed from the mealseller's steaming urn, and Kasdan brought the cups, smiling as he handed Alrathe one and frowning slightly as he handed Valdart the other. "I don't have any 'worst,' adventurer. All my supplies are equally good."

Valdart swallowed a long draft at once. "I've got my reasons," he said when he lowered the cup, as if anyone had voiced an opinion on the possible imprudence of his drinking strong morning wine in these particular circumstances. "And they don't all have to do with yesterday's brawl, either. Don't worry. I won't be the one to begin anything today."

Dilys held the fingers of one hand straight out from her cup, but sipped tea instead of speaking.

"Well, then," said the judge. "Cousin Mealcrafter, what will the damages cost you?"

"Twenty-one pebbles, two small stones and four large."

The storyteller sucked in her breath with a soft almost-whistle. "I'd hoped your first estimate was heavy, not light."

"Boken and Camys have already sold me new cushions and floormatting, and the smiths have my brazier to straighten after breakfast." Kasdan glanced at the group on the far side. "You can pay them directly if you like. Less the price of their breakfasts, which you'll pay me."

"Needlessly complicated," said the judge. "In my opinion, Cousin Kasdan, it would be simpler to pay you the whole sum. Dilys to pay fifteen pebbles, Valdart the remainder."

"What?" Valdart exclaimed.

"I have compared your four accounts with care. Dilys bears the heavier responsibility, but by treading on her leg, and by certain words spoken within her hearing and presumably the hearing of other folk, Valdart shares some measure of guilt."

"Six, almost seven pebbles' worth?" the adventurer protested.

"I'm satisfied." Dilys rose, grinned briefly at Valdart, and began counting moneygems into Kasdan's palm.

"Six pebbles, two small stones and four large," Alrathe repeated to the adventurer. "Besides what you owe for that morning wine, of course. I judge this fair."

"You barely glanced at the sum! Call in the old sky-reader, Cousin Judge. Have him knot your numbers. That's skyreaders' craft, isn't it?"

"I weighed the division last night, basing theoretical proportions on possible sums between seventeen and twenty-three pebbles. Your protests are not mannerly, Cousin Valdart," the judge added in a lower voice, "but I would like to talk with you privately in my own tent. You and Cousin Ulrad."

Ulrad seemed to quiver. "I'm sure our Cousin Judge is

being fair with the numbers, Brother Valdartin. I'm a merchant, an honest far-traveling merchant—I deal with fine goods, large numbers every day. It sounds fair to me."

"Aye," said Valdart. "Your moneypouch is snug enough, Brother Merchant."

"I'll share costs with you! Here, I'll pay it all, Brother." The merchant got his moneypouch and glanced at Alrathe. "That'll satisfy, Cousin Judge? If we pay and apologize right away for being rude to you?"

"You have not been rude to me, Cousin Ulrad. Nor have you shared any blame for the mealcrafter's expenses. You will not help Valdart pay. He needs correction in this matter and you do not." Alrathe smiled at them, thinking it would be best to get them in private immediately. "I want to speak with you both about another matter. We can breakfast afterward."

Ulrad drew his pouchstrings tight and sat kneading the money inside as if trying to wear holes in the cloth.

"Another matter," Valdart grumbled. "Well. That citron I left with you yesterday, Cousin Judge? I want it back. In good condition."

"I have it with me. But we'll speak in my tent of who should receive it back."

"I want it, and I say it's obviously mine." Then Valdart grinned awkwardly. "The truth is, Cousin Judge . . . Well, I found my pendant this morning. Snug beneath a pile of pinefeathers on my tent floor. I must've bought that citron myself sometime, set it down and forgotten to eat it."

"You have found your orangestone pendant again, safe?" Alrathe repeated. This threw the judge's calculations askelter. "But how could you forget buying a citron? Citrons are not light priced."

Valdart shrugged, that rather shamed grin still stretching his handsome face. "Maybe I still had one left from Horodek Fair. Or maybe someone gave it to me, for my charming manner. And sometimes, you know, when your lungs are full, well, your brain gets a little dizzy with all the good, boistering air and you buy something fine on impulse. Anyhow, it must be mine and I want it back."

"If it is yours, bought on giddy impulse," said the judge, "all the less reason you should balk at paying Kasdan a share of his damages. Did you find your pendant in the middle of the floor or at one side, near the tentwall?"

"At one side. Right at the edge." Valdart took another long drink of wine and frowned at the cup. "I'm lucky some little animal didn't burrow in and get it."

"And beneath a pile of pinefeathers," said the judge.

"That's right. I spread pinefeathers instead of floormatting. Some of us can't afford woven floormats."

"And some prefer not to carry the extra weight from fair to fair. Was this recovery of your pendant among the reasons you called for strong morning wine?"

"Aye. For all the joy there's left in it now."

"Will you still want to talk to us in private, Cousin Judge?" asked the merchant.

Alrathe looked from him to Valdart and the others. Dilys had counted out her payment and was lingering to finish her herbwater and be formally dismissed. Kasdan clearly hovered in wait for Valdart's share. Kara seemed to watch them with a hint of amusement from the pavilion's far side, but the group of crafters wrapped each other in their own politely quiet conversation as they breakfasted.

"No," said Alrathe. "I will not want to speak with you this morning, after all. But I will keep the citron for now. And, Cousin Valdart, I cannot direct you in this as judge, since you were complainant, but I urge you as friend to go to the toymaker and tell him yourself that your complaint against him is dissolved."

"You didn't sell anything yesterday," Nar told Torin half complainingly and half as if to make sure of the fact.

"Nothing except magic displays." The toymaker felt relaxed now that yesterday was over and today starting like a usual fair day, with his showledge set up for business outside his tent in the autumn morning sunlight. "And a few little statues I animated for the showbuyers," he added.

"Your stone turtles?"

"One." Rabbits and squirrels had been more popular.

She stared at the four tiny turtles remaining on the showledge. "The one I wanted?"

"You wanted one special turtle? I'm sorry, maybe it was. I couldn't set all my turtles aside until you came. But I'll try to animate any other one you want and not charge any extra moneygems for the magic." He reached below his ledgetop and brought out the darkring top and the turtle he had set aside for Nar at random.

"That's it! Oh, that's it!" Nar almost snatched it from his palm. "How did you know?"

"Your thoughts must have gathered around it so thickly they pulled my hand without my guessing why. I'll still try to animate it if you like."

She thought a moment and shook her head. "No. When it stopped, maybe it wouldn't be the same as it is now. With its head turned and one toe up like that. How much?"

She began digging in her pockets. Torin looked up and saw Valdart approaching.

Valdart grinned rather foolishly. Torin attempted to return the smile. Nar, unaware of the grown-ups' grins flying above her head, found a small stone, obviously hoarded with care, and handed it up to the toymaker. He gave her a large stone in change. Valdart reached the showledge.

Torin nodded. "Good morning."

"Good morning, Brother," the adventurer nodded back and waited, looking on while Torin found a bag for Nar's turtle and top.

By now the child appeared to sense something of what the men had not said to each other. No doubt, also, she had heard gossip. Taking her purchases, she said good-bye and walked away sedately, as if trying to combine manners with a lingering chance to overhear.

Torin sat, took out Arlys the metalcrafter's silverwood necklace, that she had brought him two days ago to be mended, and began carving a new snowflake link to replace the broken one. Valdart cleared his throat.

"That judgment this morning didn't come out exactly the way I'd thought it would," the adventurer said at last. "Alrathe made me pay part of the mealcrafter's damages. Almost seven pebbles. I expect that storyteller told you about it."

"A little, last night. I haven't seen her this morning."

"Oh. She didn't come by to . . . Well, never mind."

Torin was grateful Valdart stopped before saying something that might have tightened the strain on the rest of their interview. "Seven pebbles? Well, it's a good excuse for me to host you for some extra suppers this winter."

"Almost seven. So it's handy that orangestone and blue-metal pendant of mine . . . uh . . . sprouted up from beneath some pinefeathers on my tentfloor this morning."

"It did?"

Valdart caught Torin's glance and grinned. "Aye, Brother Torinel. I was surprised myself. Thought I'd sifted my floor pretty well before I started bumbling around yesterday like a bee in a patch of dried-out clover. So Cousin Judge hasn't come by to chat with you this morning, either?"

"No. I assumed you came because Alrathe assured you I hadn't taken it. So that wasn't necessary? Well, all the more reason for you to share plenty of suppers and winter evenings with me this year." Torin wanted to add, you and Sharilys, if she accepts you and if you and Dilys learn to relax in each other's company. But he still could not hope that Sharys would marry the adventurer, and Valdartak might sense the insincerity.

"Well," said Valdart, "maybe we can start by sharing a little something now? Kasdan's tent shouldn't be over-crowded, it's not midmorning yet, but my throat would welcome a little something hot and spicy. Oh, and, Torinel . . . if the little conjurer decides . . ."

"I should visit the mirror-maker anyway," said Torin. "A frame I have to return to her. I mended it in exchange for the mirror shards. And she was interested in buying a spangle-chain necklace. I'll take that along." The toymaker

smothered a sigh at breaking normal business again so
soon, and put away the metalcrafter's necklace and half-
carved new link. "Walk with me, and we'll visit Kasdan's
pavilion afterwards."

"Aye, Brother."

Valdart helped carry the showledge inside, then wandered out and waited while Torin wrapped Merprinel's
frame and necklace.

"You just mended that frame this fair?" the adventurer
asked, as if to be saying something, while Torin knitted his
charm to the doorcords. "When?"

"Early this morning. I woke before dawn and couldn't
sleep again." He must have mended Merprinel's frame
about the same time Dilys was receiving judgment. "I just
fitted in a new side to replace the cracked one, sanded it a
little and rubbed in a few drops of oil. Varnish wouldn't
have dried by tomorrow, but Merprinel almost never uses
varnished frames. Doesn't like too high a gloss around her
mirrors."

Valdart nodded sagely. They kept the conversation to
craftwork details most of the way, falling at length into a
silence that Torin thought not too uncomfortable. At least,
not until the shifting angle of their approach revealed Dilys
buying something at Merprinel's showledge.

Torin paused. He might suggest that Valdart wait for
him. Then he stepped on eagerly, the suggestion unvoiced,
leaving the old friendship to keep close or linger behind as
the old friend chose.

Before Valdart made his choice apparent, a gray mule
came careening round the corner of the Scholars' Pavilion,
knocked one post awry, caught its balance and headed toward Merprinel's tent at a gallop, eyes rolling and long
leadrope dragging.

Dilys snatched up several mirrors and jumped to one
side, Merprinel grabbed both ends of her showledge and
stood braced, Torin started forward with some vague idea
of shouting and turning the runaway's course.

But Valdart pushed him aside, ran to meet the animal

midway between the Scholars' Tent and Merprinel's, caught the leadrope at the mule's chin, laid his other hand on its neck, straightened his legs, and pulled, throating some deep, calm near-words all through the process.

They spun and whirled for a few seconds, seeming about to topple, the man dancing quickly to avoid a kick— then the mule stopped and stood, sides heaving, muscles quivering, head bobbing with teeth aimed at the leadrope, but under control.

"Adventurers' craft!" Valdart called cheerfully between measures of a song he was lulling to the animal.

"It came through the scholars' section," said the toymaker. They were hearing some shouts now, but they would have heard many more, much earlier, had it run through a craftsellers' part of the fairgrounds. "Talmar!"

"Don't run," said Valdart. "Don't startle this fellow again."

Torin walked a wide, rapid semicircle around mule and adventurer, almost bumped into the shaken tentpost, and once out of the mule's sight ran round to his brother's tent-door. Talmar and Sharys were looking out, he holding back the curtain with one arm while she insistently supported him by the other. They were gazing toward Laderan's tent at the outermost edge of the grounds, but turned at Torin's approach.

"Interesting diversion," said the high wizard. "I regret I did not have my globe outside to absorb the scene. Unfortunately, we only heard. We were not sufficiently quick to see."

"A runaway mule," Torin explained. "Someone must have been exercising it on a woods-trail, and something scared it. Valdart's stopped it safely."

"Aye. Animals follow the paths of their emotions. Unlike students." Talmar nodded and looked back at the sky-readers' tent.

Torin followed his gaze and saw that some of the shouts were plainly coming from Laderan and Iris. Their tent was distant, and they appeared smaller than statuettes, but Torin

could see the apprentice was holding something that
glinted, working it back and forth as if trying to fold or to
straighten it; and he thought Laderan's expression was
angry.

"Something broken," the toymaker guessed. "The mule
must have stepped on it. But no damage to your tent, Talmarak?"

"Only to his rest," said Sharys.

Talmar nodded. "I need rest more than plans and practice against this evening, it seems. Thank you for visiting
us, Brother. Now see whether you can earn another mon-
eystone by mending their toy."

Sharys smiled at Torin, drew Talmar inside, and closed
the doorcurtains.

Noticing Alrathe and Vathilda outside the judge's tent,
Torin stepped over to repeat his explanation of the runaway
mule Valdart had stopped.

"Aye, adventurers' work," said Vathilda, unconsciously
echoing Valdart. "Or farmcrafters' and furniture makers',
or anyone's with enough goods and business to want
wagons and beasts of their own to pull 'em. But handy that
our Valdart was there."

"Whose animal is it?" asked the judge.

"I don't know. I didn't recognize it."

"But it did no damage other than that?" Alrathe nodded
in the direction of Laderan's tent.

"A little, to one corner of the Scholars' Pavilion."

Alrathe sighed. "Well, if any new judgework grows
from this, I'll let the complainants seek me out."

"Hilshar may have more to tell us when she gets back,"
Vathilda remarked. "She misses hearing the noise, but
likely learns more through gossip about it! She's gone to
the crafters this morning to start buying those delicacies for
your brother with the money you helped us earn yesterday,
Son Toymaker. Cel's breath!"

"Cel's breath surround you," seconded the judge with a
gesture of leavetaking. Torin returned it and mentally
shook off an incipient preoccupation with why Alrathe was

interviewing Vathilda. As they retreated inside the judge's tent, he turned again toward the skyreaders'.

He approached slowly, unsure of his mannerliness yet remembering that sometimes a disinterested third party could help quiet these angerslides. He did not, however, get the chance to attempt crafting calm between them. Hesitating when he came near enough to make out their words clearly, he heard Iris say,

"But I keep telling you I didn't leave it outside to be rid of it! I just forgot! I was overtired from helping all day at their magic show and I just forgot to bring it in!" Her voice choked. "And now I've cut my finger and it's bleeding. Here!" She thrust the broken thing into Laderan's hands and pushed past him into the tent.

Torin walked up more quickly, guessing he might help by ensuring that the old skyreader remain separated from his apprentice for a few moments.

"Obvious to any fool it wasn't a mirror to study with," Laderan muttered. He turned to the newcomer. "Here, toy-crafter, can you fix this?"

Torin shifted Merprinel's bundle, which he had carried safe more by instinct than thought, and took what Laderan held out. It had been a small brownish-tinted mirror in a goldenwood frame. Two sides of the frame were crushed and little more than a third of the pane still clung, fragmented, to the sides left whole. Torin thought he remembered seeing it among Merprinel's new showpieces earlier this season.

"I could mend the frame. I'd have to carve two new sides. And I'm sure Merprinel could replace the mirror. But it'd cost almost as much as you paid for it new."

"Not worth it. New yesterday. Clear she didn't care about it." Tears were running down Laderan's crinkled cheeks.

"It's good wood," said Torin. "I think I could get quite a few inlay chips out of the broken sides. I'd credit you for the wood and the mirror shards. That'd make the job less expensive."

"I gave it to her yesterday. She had it out playing with it last night. Any fool could see it wasn't made for sky-reading work. And she left it out. Not worth fixing. Take it, toymaker. Don't mend the thing, take it and welcome to it."

He turned away and started walking toward the woods. Torin shifted Merprinel's bundle beneath his arm again, picked up several shining fragments from the ground, wrapped them with the rest of the mirror in his handycloth, and returned to the other side of the Scholars' Pavilion.

A small crowd had gathered, among them Merchant Kara, who strode through to join Valdart from one direction as Torin rejoined him from the other, in the area folk were leaving clear around the animal.

"Aye," Kara said grimly. "That's my mule. Trask."

Trask nickered and swung his head toward Kara at mention of his name. She caught the leadrope harness at his cheek and turned the small, wooden owner's disk back to the side that had her 'K' burned in the local alphabet. "Vittor," she went on in a low, barely contained voice. "He has their morning care today. He's let this happen once too often, exercising more animals than he can control at a time. How much damage?"

"One corner of the Scholars' Pavilion, and this mirror." Torin partially unwrapped it, careful not to let any possible sunglint catch the mule's line of vision. "I think that's all."

Kara looked at the broken mirror and nodded for him to wrap it up again. "Vittor will come to pay, probably within the hour. I assume Mother Vathilda, as senior scholar here, will collect for damage to the pavilion. Whose mirror was it?"

"The skyreader bought it yesterday." Torin paused. "And gave it to his apprentice the same day. I'm not sure. He paid, but it was hers by the time Trask's hoof hit it."

"Merprinel's work? We'll find out its price from her. Vittor will deliver half to each skyreader and they can put it together or divide it otherwise as they decide." Kara smiled. "Cousin Alrathe compared us far-traveling merchants to skyreaders, for our calculations and number-knotting. We also learn to be judges to our hired adventurers. It's necessary on our travels, and thrifty when we're in settled neighborhoods."

"Learn a little magic, and you can wear any color student's robe," said Valdart.

She looked at him and smiled again. "Maybe I know a little magic already, Brother. You've traveled farther east and west, but I've traveled farther north and south. Now lead Trask back to the animal enclosure, take Vittor's place for the rest of the morning, and I'll give you a full morning's pay, no matter how you decide afterwards."

"Happily, Cousin Kara." Valdart grinned. Then, "Uh, Torinel, suppose we share that little refreshment this afternoon?"

"Between midday and twilight. I'll watch for you."

Valdart led the mule away, and the crowd started dispersing. Kara and Torin crossed to Merprinel's booth, where Dilys waited, smiling, a smallish, flat carrying-bag tucked beneath one elbow.

Merprinel sighed when she saw the broken mirror. "Two pebbles and three large stones," she answered Kara's question about its price.

"Almost what I had guessed," replied the merchant.

"So your mule broke one of my pieces after all," the mirror-maker went on. "It's always melancholy to see craftwork spoiled."

Kara looked at the showledge. "Fortunate for Vittor that mule didn't reach your unsold stock. His moneypouch is not likely to gather any more gems from mine." She wished them good-bye and left.

"Poor Vittor," Dilys said softly.

"Yes." Torin felt grateful he was himself, with the hard climbing of these last two days below him, rather than Vittor with discomfort ahead. "But Kara remarked it's not the first time he's been careless. Apparently she'd warned him. Well, I'll pay him for the reusable wood and mirror fragments." He gave Merprinel her mended frame and showed her the silverlink necklace. "This is priced at a pebble and one small stone."

"Well worth the price. Yes, I will buy it."

While Merprinel got her money, Torin turned back to Dilys. "How does your throat feel?"

"Much better. I may be able to tell my stories this afternoon." She linked her free arm through his. "If I slip something else hot down it this morning. Sip with me?"

That afternoon shortly before Valdart arrived, Iris came to the toymaker's booth. "Brother Torin, do you still have my mirror?"

He did not ask how long she had practiced before she could call him "brother" after so many seasons of teasing him with "son." "Yes. I've already paid Vittor the adventurer what the usable materials are worth, Sister Iris."

"That's all right. He paid Uncle Laderan and me." She drew in a shaky breath. "But I do want it mended."

"I'd have to charge almost a pebble for the frame, and Merprinel would probably want another pebble for the new mirror. That's nearly as much as Laderan paid for it new."

"Yes. I know. Uncle Laderan gave me all Vittor's repayment. He insisted I take it. Brother Toymaker, I do want my mirror. Not a new one to replace it. That one."

"All you'll really have of the original will be half its frame." And Torin would lose by the arrangement, since he had paid Vittor for those two whole sides as well as the fragments, and in kindness and fairness he saw no way to ask anyone for that amount back. But, looking at Iris, he suggested, "I think I could work some pieces of the original mirror into the frame design as inlay, if you like."

"I'd like that. Yes, I think I'd like it very much. Thank you, Brother Torivin."

"Well, you'd better tell Merprinel. Here." He picked out a long, thin shard and gave it to Iris. "In case she needs it to match the tint more exactly. I can't have the frame mended by tomorrow, you understand."

"I understand! Horodek Icecrystal Fair? Or maybe I can come to your shop before then?"

"Give me at least twelve days."

"Thank you, Brother," she repeated. "Cel surround you."

Fifteen

TORIN AND DILYS came to see Talmar's magic display together. Their long friendship was sufficient explanation. They had watched closing shows side by side at numerous fairs. When Sharys was a child, she had sometimes stood on a stepladder between them. If she guessed tonight they had found something besides friendship . . . It might not be so ungentle an intimation.

Vathilda, Hilshar, and Sharys were also among the early arrivals in the audience circle this evening. The highest ranking magicker always climbed the platform outside the Scholars' Pavilion alone on the last night. Once there, the magicker used a mind-message to summon an assistant: this was the first of seven feats fixed by tradition. Ideally, no one should know ahead of time who that assistant would be (though sometimes, when the magicker was low ranking and not adept at mind-messages, they arranged it beforehand), but most often a fellow magicker or other student was chosen, occasionally a storycrafter. Torin and Dilys hoped the high wizard would not summon either of them tonight.

When she saw them, Vathilda left the stool on which she had been sitting and joined them to gossip. "I think he'll call our Sharys," she confided, not happily. "I told him I didn't want it. Better have me or my daughter by him in case he glory-chokes again. Experience! More likely to seed her with boasting sickness, if everything goes as he plans. But she keeps silent about it, just nods and grins." The old sorceress peered at Dilys and Torin and shook her head. "Well, what was all that fuss-over about the mule this morning, eh? We heard it was Merchant Kara's animal and she's unhired one of her adventurers because of it. He wouldn't say much about it himself. Only paid us for damages."

"He'd taken three of her pack animals out to exercise at once," Torin explained somewhat reluctantly. Valdart had recounted the tale to him that afternoon. "A snake startled one of them, the first one startled the others, and while he was holding two, one broke away."

"It was the fourth time he let something of the kind happen." Kara had come up behind them, and showed no reluctance to add further explanation. "I told him to look for work on a ship or in a mealshop, not with animals. Cel's breath." She passed on to lean against a tentpost.

Vathilda grunted. "I'm not sure I'd trust that one to trade with. . . . Laderan bought himself some harvest colors today. A belt as wide as his midfinger's long. They've talked it through, and the sapling plans to stay and work with him when she's full skyreader—as niece and uncle. We'll see where they are next amberleaf season. Alrathe wants you and Valdart tomorrow morning, Son Toycrafter. And my granddaughter wants you in our tent after the high wizard's performance. Whether he's still healthy or not, she says."

Valdart was coming into the audience area. The sorceress took her leave of them with a nod and moved on to him.

"Sharys will want only you and Valdart," the storycrafter murmured. "And maybe someone else, but not me.

I wonder if Cousin Alrathe will let me in with you tomorrow morning?"

The crows gathered, mingled, eddied about to exchange greetings. Every fairgoer attended, even Kasdan, his daughter and their young apprentice Perlyn, although they stood on the outer fringe so as to hurry back and reopen their meal tent immediately after the display. Talmar alone was late. At this season, the traditional first tricks should be performed as sun touched horizon. East'dek's fairground being ringed by forest, the horizon was hidden, but the sun dissolved until it cast no more shadows, the clear sky above the treetops deepened to sapphire, and Torin was beginning to worry. Nor was he the only one, by certain signs of tension in the audience. Sharys, however, seemed calm, as nearly as he could still see her expression in the twilight.

At last the curtains behind the platform swished apart and the high wizard slowly climbed the steps. By now, the sky was nearly the same shade as his dark azure robe. Except for a black streak at either temple, he had silvered his hair. It was a permissible effect for any magic-monger who had at least seven natural gray strands, and Talmar's thick hair had begun dappling early even for a scholar. Nevertheless, Torin thought the hint of long, lingering illness, combined with the suggestion of a mage's silver head, slightly pretentious.

Talmar carried his globe. Unlit, it remained scarcely visible against his robe, so that he seemed almost to pantomime when he set it down on his table. Next he brought a thin white rope from his sleeve, waggled it so that all could see how supple it was, and transformed it into a metal stand, twice as tall as the rope's natural length. He set his globe atop the stand. If his transformation were weak and unknit itself unexpectedly, he risked losing the precious sphere.

He gestured with unnecessary extravagance and the globe burst into light—white, clear and dazzling for a moment, then settling to lucent silkiness.

All this was before the traditional summoning of an assistant that should have opened this display, yet Talmar had slipped it in as preparation, and his audience responded with a two-line song.

Now the high wizard closed his eyes, and the globe sent out rays of colored light. This was rarely seen in any but mages' displays, and Torin had only heard of its being coupled with the summoning twice, both times by elder mages. The rays began revolving, faster and faster, red, orange, gold, green, blue, purple, and white flickering after one another. Had the revolution been a few heartbeats faster or the colors a tone more bright, it would have caused eye-ache. Indeed, Torin wondered if his brother were truly combining light control with summons, or if the actual mind-message would come slightly afterwards, in a gap when most of the audience had finally closed their eyes.

No. Torin's gaze was on Kara only by chance at the moment, but he saw her stiffen and glance up in the middle of the light show. Gold, green, and blue moved across her face as she stared upward, but despite the color distortion her surprise was obvious. As blue changed to purple, she shrugged, moved away from her tentpost, and began looking about the ground.

A far-traveling merchant, a relative stranger seen in this neighborhood every third year, was an unusual choice for assistant. The audience whispered a little as more and more of them saw whom Talmar had summoned. Torin managed to exchange a glance with Sharys; it told him she was not disappointed. She must have known Talmar would not choose her.

If Kara's morning quip to Valdart about knowing a snatch of magic had been more than idle joking, any small feats she knew would probably belong to the different techniques of far-away places. And no one who had seen Kara's reaction would believe she had known ahead of time. The display was to be entirely of Talmar's skill, with only minimal and nonmagical help from his assistant, not the combination of power that conjurers and magicians sometimes resorted to.

Kara found a fallen twig with numerous dry leaves still attached, picked it up and carried it to the platform. She climbed the steps and gave Talmar the twig. His light-spectrum dissolved into a steady milk-white tinged with gold. He cupped his hands over the twig for an instant, opened them, and a stream of white throstlebirds flew up from between his fingers, chirruping their six-note garland of song.

This was another traditional transformation, though in autumn and winter shows the species of birds, the base materials, and the exact place in the schedule were left to the performer's choice. Usually eggs were involved and the birds a colorful variety of species sent flying into tawny sky above a sun not quite vanished. Tonight they fluttered a moment around the platform, all white and seemingly almost as delicate as dried leaves catching the globelight, then rose like flakes of snow, or glowing white ash, or stars falling upward into a blue tourmaline sky. Torin wondered if such an effect could ever be captured in the static craftwork of wood and stone.

When the birds had disappeared, Talmar transformed the leafless twig into a miniature tree of metallic gold. Holding it with thumb and forefinger on top of his globe, he embellished it by causing gem-sparkling leaves and fruits to grow and unfold on its fine branches. When he took his hand away, the tree remained fixed to the globe.

So the display continued, seven feats determined at least in their outline by tradition, seven left completely to choice. Almost every traditional feat Talmar stamped with details of his own. Interspersed with these new effects, most of his selected tricks seemed comparatively mild. But always he used his globelight for greatest enhancement, now one color, now another, a spectrum between every two tricks, spinning sometimes one way and sometimes another, the golden tree reflecting additional glitters over the scene.

During the traditional last feat, making and spellcasting a protective charm for the assistant, he kept the entire spectrum revolving at a speed just slow enough for eye comfort. He proved the power of his new disk by tying it around his fingers and holding his own hand in flame for several minutes. For the first time that evening he failed to win an enthusiastic short song. That any magicker would risk natural flesh in such demonstration was unheard of. Even use of creatures temporarily transformed from inanimate material was unpopular, and half or more of the audience watched the turning shafts of light instead of the high wizard. But they agreed that Kara gained a protective charm which would not need renewing for years.

Talmar had performed fourteen tricks, the customary number, and that was not counting his preliminary business with rope and globe. But before his audience, still shocked by his last feat of hand in fire, could begin their concluding song he held out both arms and declaimed:

"Cousins and friends! You may have heard gossip of my newest technique. You may have heard that I can make my globe show again, in reverse, whatever it has caught in reflection. Unable to demonstrate this to all of you at once in its fine detail, I have designed my entire display to demonstrate it on a larger scale."

He held up a large, round wooden tray, transformed it into a mirror, and set it flat on the table. Taking his globe from its rope-stand, he removed the miniature gold tree, turning the sphere upside down, set it on the mirror, and made his new series of gestures over it.

All the colors it had spun during his performance began to repeat in reverse, bouncing up re-echoed and magnified by the mirror. Talmar replaced the little tree on what was now the globe's top, and the glister of gold and tiny jewels doubled and repeated itself. He transformed numerous smaller mirrors, arranged them vertically around the large one, added a candle here, a small shell-sided lantern there. Colors and spangles flowed around the audience like a strange blizzard of tints and flames, almost tangible enough to feel.

Dilys held Torin close. "The ancients may have had something like this," she murmured, very softly so as not to disturb the general hush. "Colored blossoms of fire that burst apart in the night sky and showered down without doing any harm. I wondered if it could have been so lovely?"

He returned her hug.

Talmar folded his arms at last and stood looking down at his audience through the play of lights, smiling as they finally began to applaud. They repeated the long song twice. The high wizard showed not the least difficulty in breathing.

Sixteen

TORIN HAD COME to her tent last night. Dilys waited in his tonight. She fingered what she had bought from Merprinel that morning, twice taking it out of its soft-lined bag to look at it again. And once she picked up the statue of Ilfting and the Brightwings, the one Torin said might have come to life and spoken two nights ago. She could not understand why Kara and Ulrad had both wanted Ilfting and his porcupines, while neither had taken Ilfting and the Brightwings. This one, she thought, was better crafted, and the tale more widely known. She had invented the story of the three porcupines herself, and so far as she knew it had not yet traveled beyond Bavardek. But the statue Kara had bought was much smaller and lighter.

Torin came in. At first she could not quite read his expression in the candlelight. Happy, but not perfectly unmixed.

"Torinel? Whom did she choose?"

"Talmar." He sat beside her on the bed. They each put an arm around the other, and he laughed softly. "Neither one of us, neither Valdart nor me. Thank Cel, not me! My brother Talmar."

Dilys was unsurprised. "I expected it. Didn't you, seeing them in his tent yesterday evening?"

"We both more or less expected it. Her mother, her grandmother, Cousin Alrathe, probably they all saw it even sooner. Valdart must have been the only one who never suspected. It seems he was simply her infatuation. As she was mine. We were both ripe for marriage, Sharilys and I, and the wrong newcomer stood in our moonlight to keep us from seeing the old companion for a while."

"Fortunate for everyone none of you made it permanent. Though I still think she would have been more comfortable with you than with Valdart. . . . How did he accept her choice?"

Torin sighed deeply. "Someday he might understand. He didn't tonight. He told me if I hadn't advised her to wait, she'd have married him and been happy. Then he left Vathilda's tent, alone. I didn't try to follow him."

"Wise."

"At least he said it quietly, so she wouldn't overhear, and walked out slowly."

"That promises healing."

"Sharys probably doesn't guess that she was only my infatuation, either." He grinned. "You should have watched her being as gentle as possible with me, Dilysin. I don't think she has any idea how comfortable I am with her choice. She should have concentrated more on being gentle with Valdartak."

Too gentle with that adventurer, Dilys thought, and he might not have believed it. Asked which of the two she judged more susceptible to boasting sickness, Dilys would say Valdart rather than the high wizard. But that was nothing to tell Torin. "Valdart was already an excellent storyteller, Torinel," she said. "This could make him even better. Good enough so that, if he does decide to stop adventuring, he'll be able to slip into true storycrafting with a year's late apprenticeship."

"Will all this make you a better storycrafter, too?"

"The wine-brawl will, I think." She teased him a little. "More than almost losing you to Sharilys." She had climbed over the worst of that long before this Amberleaf Fair. "But you had a long infatuation, Torinel. Half a year."

"Too long. It would have been shorter if I'd offered her my marriage toy sooner."

"But then she might have taken it." Dilys slipped away from Torin long enough to get her carrying-bag. Snuggling close again, she unwrapped her purchase and laid it across both their knees. It was one of Merprinel's finest mirrors, a double square of gold-tinted panes in blackwood frame embellished with gold leaf and ivory. The squares joined at one point, the joining so deep and clever that neither square seemed to lose a point. Dilys might not have felt she could afford it had she not earned extra moneygems thanks to this fair's gossip, and had she not had to pay the mealseller less than she'd expected. But it made the perfect marriage token.

"Let me pay half whatever this cost," said Torin after a moment. "That way, it can be both our token to one another."

That struck her as a beautiful idea. "All right. On condition that when the time comes you carve my birthing-bed charm yourself."

They went to the crimson tent together next morning. All over the rest of the ground fairgoers were starting to pack their possessions and fold their tents, but the scholars' corner was still quiet. After a clear night, the two sky-readers would sleep until midday.

Alrathe was sitting outside, watching brazier and kettle.

"I'm sure you intend to tell them the true tale of Valdart's glitterstone, Cousin," said Dilys. "Do you mind if I hear it direct from you at the same time? I did help Torin list those foods to help you solve the puzzle of Talmar's illness."

"Aye, the puzzles intertwine," replied the judge. "I see no reason you should not stay, Cousin Storycrafter."

Valdart came soon after. The valleys beneath his eyes were not as dark as might have been feared. Apparently he had begun to recover from his disappointment in time to get half a night's sleep. He drew back on seeing Dilys, then shrugged and came forward again with something of his old strut.

They went inside for added privacy, Torin and Valdart carrying brazier and kettle. Alrathe motioned them to sit and poured three cups of hot herbwater. Torin recognized one of the cups as borrowed from Vathilda.

"None for me, Cousin Judge," said Valdart. "Uh . . . Cousin Kara wants to leave as early as possible." He grinned at Torin. "She offered yesterday to hire me in Vittor's place. I . . . After Sharys chose your brother the wizard, I decided to accept Kara's offer. I guess that means no shared suppers and winter evenings after all, this year."

"They'll be waiting when you visit our neighborhood again." Three years as Kara's hired adventurer might smooth away the traces of rockslide better than any other remedy.

Valdart cleared his throat and nodded. "Aye. Well, I'm grateful for a few minutes of leavetaking. So, Cousin Judge, if you'll explain things . . . like a story."

Alrathe took the third cup of herbwater, sipped from it, and began. "The first puzzle was Talmar's illness. The second was the appearance of the high wizard's globe in Torin's tent, the third the disappearance of the orangestone pendant from Valdart's. All these incidents were bound together. A seeming fourth puzzle shook my confidence in my own reasoning yesterday morning when Valdart's pendant reappeared, but it proved to be only a natural outgrowth.

"We already know how Talmar's illness, which Mother Vathilda thought glory-choking, turned out to be simple sensitivity to a rather uncommon combination of foods. And Talmar made no secret of having sent his own globe to his brother in what he then believed a deathbed message to win the last of his family back to the family study.

"Talmar would not, however, name his messenger, at the messenger's own insistence. It could only have been someone who was near him that afternoon, since when we left him alone to wait for the Harvest Spirit, who wisely decided to pass him by, he was too weak to have summoned anyone over a distance.

"It was not Torin, by logic and the workings of mind-messages as well as by Talmar's own assurance. I saw no reason why any of the students, Vathilda, her family, and the skyreaders, should have desired such secrecy, unless in a spirit of teasing, and that did not fit the seriousness of Talmar's condition. But I remembered that one other had stepped briefly into the Scholars' Tent that afternoon, coming in with Iris on the pretext of unfinished business with the toymaker—"

"Ulrad!" Torin exclaimed. "And we assumed Talmar sent him a mind-message to leave him in quiet."

Alrathe nodded. "Ulrad must have come partly in curiosity and partly because he did have unfinished business with the toymaker. Talmar did indeed send the merchant a mind-message, but it was to come to him that night if he should be alone in his tent. At the moment, Talmar probably had only a confused idea of the use he would make of Ulrad, but Torin had already shown resistance to magic and to taking the globe.

"By the time Ulrad came that night, Talmar knew he would use him to deliver the globe, but he had to explain the trick of getting past Torin's doorcharm: That such charms work only to keep mischief away and do not sense intention to bring harmless items inside as mischievous. Since all he planned was leaving Talmar's globe in Torin's tent, Ulrad could slip under the doorcord as easily as his bulk allowed, or even untie and retie it afterward.

"Ulrad must have guessed at once that the charm might recognize unauthorized trade as no more mischievous than a deposited gift. That would be why he made Talmar prom-

ise to keep his identity secret. No doubt the wizard thought
this secrecy foolishness, but he saw no reason not to promise, and kept his promise faithfully once it was made.

"Ulrad had particularly coveted Valdart's pendant for
most of this season, and he surely had enough experience
to guess what even I was able to work out in an interview
with Kara: That in theory, somewhere, a citron and an
orangestone pendant might be worth the same price. Perhaps Ulrad concentrated on this theory all the while he
entered Valdart's tent and made the exchange, or perhaps
our doorcharms have no sense whatever of comparative
values. In any case, the citron was a genuine citron.

"I had reasoned all this very nearly as I've told it, and
strongly suspected Ulrad to be the culprit, but he must have
guessed my suspicions, or his own nervousness wore him
down, especially after his involvement—innocent though
his part was—in the wine-brawl between Valdart and
Dilys. Knowing he must be present next morning for my
final judgment in that case, and fearing I might take the
opportunity to bring out his own guilt in the more serious
matter, which I had indeed intended to do privately right
afterward, he returned to Valdart's tent in the night. This
time he merely slipped his hand beneath the tentwall and
left the pendant under the pinefeathers."

"That footstep we heard that night!" said Dilys. "It
might have been Ulrad."

Valdart glanced at her, probably realizing that by "we"
she meant herself and Torin. The adventurer shrugged,
half-smiled, and nodded.

"When Valdart told us of the pendant's reappearance,"
the judge went on, "I naturally had to sort through and
retest my theory. I consulted Vathilda, who agreed that my
reasoning had been sound and in accordance with the facts
of our neighborhood's magic. Then I visited Ulrad. Fortunately, he had not dared leave a day early, for fear of rous-
ing further suspicion. In his extreme nervousness, he
confessed everything after a question or two—everything,

I mean, except a few private thought processes which I saw little reason to probe more exactly."

"What correction did you give the sneak thief?" Valdart asked grimly.

Alrathe produced the citron, two moneypouches, and two large bottles. "Ten pebbles' worth of moneygems and a bottle of rarespice cordial apiece to Valdart and Torin for the mental discomfort and strain to old friendship. Valdart also keeps the citron. Since Ulrad himself returned the pendant, and since he suffered great nervous anguish, I judged the cost of these repayments sufficient correction. He is not likely to attempt such mischief again, so the correction will have served its purpose. And as long as he behaves whenever in our neighborhood, I have promised him secrecy for the sake of his honest business. I believe he was probably among the first to depart this morning."

Valdart took his moneypouch, bottle, and citron, counted the moneygems, unstoppered the bottle to drink a few swallows, declared it excellent stuff, and got to his feet. "Well, Cousin Judge. I'd have asked two or three bottles of this stuff, but . . ."

"You owe me a pebble for my judgment," Alrathe said quietly.

"What? But I cancelled my complaint yesterday morning."

"Nevertheless, you were the complainant who led me to discover a culprit and whose property might not have been returned if not for my probing."

"Cousin Alrathe," said Torin, "I'll pay the pebble."

"Valdart will pay it," replied the judge. "It may help him remember to think more carefully before bringing another complaint. Had you contented yourself with reporting your loss, Cousin Adventurer . . . but you also accused an innocent person specifically and rashly. You were more responsible than Ulrad for your friend's discomfort."

"In that case," said the adventurer, "why don't I pay Torinel the pebble?"

Alrathe nodded.

"Good." Valdart turned to Torin. "Take this cordial instead of the pebble, Chosen Brother. Too big a bottle for me to pack along. We'd just drink it right away along the road."

Torin accepted the bottle, intending to give it to Alrathe when Valdart was gone.

"Well, Torinel." The adventurer rubbed the toymaker's shoulder. "We'll say our right good-byes for this time when I come to the old neighborhood again. Just before we say our greetings."

"Valdartak."

Valdart turned and left, eating his citron.

Alrathe refused the whole bottle, but did take two small glasses of its contents to help Dilys and Torin celebrate their marriage.